The Body in the Blackberries

A Callum Lange Mystery

Nicola Pearson

This story is a work of fiction.
No part of the contents relate to any real person or persons, living or dead.

ISBN-13: 978-1721084036

ISBN-10: 1721084037

Acknowledgments

I don't think I would ever have been able to write about nature the way I do if it weren't for the details I hear from my husband's retelling of his walks in the mountains around our home. I thank him, with all my heart, for opening my eyes to the natural world. I would also like to thank my editor Kirsten Colton, for making sure the details I pass along in this mystery are clear for those who don't necessarily wander the wilderness, and for her other, helpful corrections. Thanks also to my longtime editor Jerry Ziegler, for his continued encouragement, and to my friend Jay Wisman, who let me pick his brain about the law. For the policing details I am once again indebted to Detective Theresa Luvera, who also pointed me toward the very knowledgeable and helpful Skagit County coroner, Haley Thompson, as well as to Burlington Police Chief, Mike Luvera. And finally, my thanks to Amanda Knudtsen for answering some questions but mostly for being such a lovely inspiration.

Cover Art

Original photograph of Sauk Mountain in spring by Jude Dippold; watercolor painting of a wild blackberry vine by Doris Pollack; graphic design by Jon-Paul Verfaillie

For my son, Reed,
who loves these mountains.

CHAPTER 1

Lange was pounding down Sauk Mountain Road in the heat of the midmorning when he suddenly became aware of something beside him. He startled so fiercely his whole body jumped. *"You scared the shit out of me!"* he yelled at the blonde in the silver Range Rover, which had appeared without him hearing it approach *at all.*

"I'm so sorry," said the driver, her brow wrinkled over her big blue eyes.

Lange felt his hostility evaporate, especially when he noticed her lush pink lips. He felt a tug inside him, something he hadn't felt for a long time.

"Might you be Callum Lange?" asked the blonde.

"I might," Lange offered. "It depends on who you might be."

The blonde chuckled, obviously not bothered by Lange's wariness.

"I'm Agent Pate-Swenson, with the DEA," said the blonde, showing him her badge.

"The DEA?" Lange exclaimed. "What in the world is the DEA doing all the way out here in the middle of nowhere?"

"The middle of nowhere is where small planes like to drop drugs they've flown in from Canada."

Which triggered something in Lange's mind. "A small *plane*," he mused out loud. That would explain it.

The agent propped her left elbow on the open window and leaned toward Lange, obviously curious about the connection he'd just made. "Did you see one?"

"Er, no, well, I mean, no, I didn't 'see' anything . . ." Lange said, rattled. She was leaning close enough that he could smell her perfume, and he liked it so well he couldn't focus. He swung left because for some reason he needed to look down the road, and felt his synapses clear, putting him back on point. "It's just," he went on, "the other morning I heard a noise, and I couldn't quite place it." His eyes narrowed as he thought back to the moment. "It was early, not yet six, I want to say, and I was writing at my desk in the middle of the yurt, listening to a podcast . . ."

"Which one?" asked the agent.

"What's that?" Lange made eye contact with her again. "Oh. *Serial*."

Pate-Swenson nodded, like she knew it. "Detectiving even when you're not detectiving," she remarked.

"It helps me switch my brain off so I can concentrate," Lange explained. "Anyway, the podcast had some distracting background sounds in it, so I wasn't sure if the noise I thought I heard was coming from that or from outside. But now that you mention it, it did sound like a small plane."

"Did you go investigate?"

"What? The noise?" Lange shook his head. "No, because I wasn't sure I'd heard anything."

"Have you noticed anything out of the ordinary since you heard it? Which was when, by the way?"

"Monday."

"So yesterday."

"If today's Tuesday, that would be correct."

"I guess I meant Monday of this week? It could have been last week."

"You're right." Lange thought for a moment. "But no, it was yesterday. I guess I don't really pay attention to the days, living out here."

"So have you seen anything unusual since then?"

"What? Here on the road, d'you mean?"

"Yes. Maybe when you were out for your walk?"

Lange wanted to say, *How did you know . . . ?* but there was something very disarming about the way Pate-Swenson was looking at him. "Did I notice anything unusual . . . ?" he repeated. He had taken a walk on Monday, to blow the cobwebs out of his brain, so he retraced his steps in his mind. He stopped, remembering something. "There's this place just off the road, beyond one of the big logging-company gates, where I like to pick wild blackberries. Those are the tiny ones that come on early," he explained. "They call them dewberries up here, sometimes tanglefoot berries because they grow on vines that sprawl across the ground and the sidehills. Anyway, I walked in yesterday to see if the berries were ripe yet, since this July has been so hot, and I do remember thinking that the hillside above the patch that I was examining looked disturbed."

"In what way?"

"There were bent and broken branches, like something had gone through them. I'd seen a pile of bear scat, so I assumed it was the bear foraging in the berries, but"—he shrugged—"it could have been a shipment of drugs dropped from the sky." Lange visualized the patch of brush, trying to remember if he'd seen anything down in amongst the brambles. But he hadn't. He'd been too focused on sampling the ripe berries.

The DEA agent's face remained passive. "Can you take me there?" she asked.

"Sure," Lange replied. He respected her ability to hide her reactions. "It's not that much farther down the road. You can follow me if you like."

"Why don't you hop in?" Pate-Swenson said, tapping the seat beside her with her right hand.

Lange felt caught off guard again. "Umm, well, I was . . . I guess I . . . erm . . . what's your name again?"

"Pate-Swenson," said the agent. She smiled. "But you can call me Michelle."

"Michelle," repeated Lange, glad to know her first name. He was immediately embarrassed that he'd said it out loud and hastened around the front of the vehicle, climbing in without making eye contact. As soon as he reached for the seat belt, he felt something warm on the back of his neck. Lange jumped for the second time that morning.

He spun around to find himself nose to nose with a large German shepherd. "What the . . . ?!"

"Oh, that's Kojak," said Michelle. "He won't hurt you."

Lange peered over his shoulder at the canine, who didn't seem the least bit interested in him, having eyes only for his mistress. Smart dog, thought Lange. "Can I pet him?" he asked.

"Oh sure. He's very friendly. Unless you're carrying drugs, of course."

"He's a working K9 then?" said Lange, as he let the pup smell his hand.

"Not anymore. He's retired. Aren't you, Kojak?"

The dog made a couple of talky whining sounds, as if he were answering. Lange studied him. He looked vibrantly healthy, with shiny dark eyes and a coat that was reminiscent of natural amber with its mix of honey browns, grays, and gold. "He's got a lot of hair for a Kojak."

"Yeah, but . . . who loves ya, baby?" joked Michelle.

Lange couldn't help but grin, too. "They don't mind you bringing your dog to ride along even if he's not at work?"

"I only bring him when I come this far up the mountain. Just in case I meet any strange men," Michelle replied. She glanced at him, her eyes full of mischief.

Was she flirting with him? he wondered. Or was that just her natural way of being? He half closed one eye and twitched his head repeatedly. "You find me strange?" he said in a deep Frankenstein's monster voice.

Michelle laughed.

"Okay, slow down," said Lange as they approached a wide turn in the Forest Service road. He knew that the long tubular yellow gate was set back from this turn.

Michelle slowed to a crawl, the Range Rover lurching in and out of the potholes on the uphill side of the road.

"This is where we get out," said Lange, pointing across at the gate.

Michelle pulled into the wide, brushy apron in front of the gate. Nature had taken over again here, and the tires crunched through ankle-high grass and dry twigs as she swung her vehicle around to park in the shade of the tall conifers. "D'you mind if I bring Kojak?" she asked. She switched off the engine and took the keys out of the ignition.

It was mid-morning and still quite early in July, but the day was already heating up and Lange could imagine how uncomfortable the dog would be cooped up in the vehicle. "Not at all," he replied. He opened his door to step out and heard Michelle click twice in her cheek. He looked back to see the shepherd bound across the driver's seat and out the door after his mistress. Lange and Michelle slammed their doors and moved in unison toward the low gate.

Kojak raced ahead of them, ducking his narrow form easily under the lowest bar on the gate. He cantered down the abandoned logging road, his tail swinging happily behind him. Lange and Michelle edged around the gate, then fell in step on both sides of the pearly everlastings growing down the center of the road. The white herbaceous wildflowers were almost to Lange's hip.

"Is that where you were?" Michelle asked, pointing forward at the German shepherd, who had stopped running a hundred feet ahead of them by a small fir tree lying across the road.

"No, the berries are farther along," said Lange.

"Well, he's found something to sniff."

"Probably that bear scat."

They caught up with the dog and hiked their legs over the fallen tree. Michelle clicked in her cheek again for Kojak to follow. The dog raced after them, passed them, then came to a screeching halt a good hundred yards farther. He picked across the blackberry vines growing out of the uphill side of the road, sniffing the whole way, and suddenly stopped, his body taut, his coat shimmering in the sunlight as if from excitement, his right front leg poised to spring up the hillside.

"Kojak, *stay*!" Michelle shouted, speeding up beside Lange. The dog set his paw back on the ground, but his nose was bumping the air with alacrity. "That the spot?" she asked.

"Exactly."

"Down," commanded Michelle. The dog lowered himself, eyes back on his mistress. "I just don't want him to disturb what you saw," she explained to Lange.

Within seconds they were next to Kojak, and Michelle snapped her fingers for him to heel, all the while praising him in a soft, high-pitched voice. The dog came to her left side and stayed close as she moved her eyes slowly this way and that.

Lange sniffed; there was a faint scent of warm berries in the air and something else. Something that was nudging a memory.

Michelle interrupted him before he could place it. She was looking uphill now. "Were you referring to those smashed-down ferns?" she asked.

Lange nodded. "Yes." He pointed across her. "And that wild cherry has some hanging limbs."

"Uh-huh," agreed Michelle. She tipped her head back to see the sky. "If a large delivery of drugs dropped from a plane overhead, could that have caused such a trail through the brush?"

"It's possible," said Lange. "Depending on how it fell. Although I see what you're getting at. It does seem to have made a fairly wide swath." Which made him think. "I wonder if the package landed in the ditch, under the blackberries?"

He stepped forward and looked down. Instantly he saw that it wasn't a shipment of drugs that had landed in the blackberries. And he knew what that smell was.

"Is that a body?" came Michelle's voice from beside him.

Behind them, Kojak tipped his head back and let out an anguished howl.

CHAPTER 2

"**W**hat in the world put you there, Robert?" Lange asked, looking down at the old fellow who'd met his end at the side of a logging road.

"You know this man?"

Lange nodded. "That's Robert Doyle. I bought some lumber from him to lay under my yurt when I set it up. He seemed like a real straight-ahead guy."

Michelle sighed. "It's not usually straight-ahead guys that get messed up in drug trafficking."

Lange crouched, saddened by the fact that this seemingly innocuous old fellow, with his close-cropped buzz of white hair and thin, elderly frame, had met such a lonely end. A violent end, too, if the angry-looking bruise on the left side of his face was anything to go by. Now that he was down low, peering through all the undergrowth growing out of the ditch and into the road, he noticed the flies drawn by the body. Lange swatted them away with his hand. "I'm stunned that I didn't see him yesterday," he said to Michelle, who was taking photos of the scene with her phone. "You'd've thought I'd see his red checked shirt if nothing else."

"This is where you were eating blackberries yesterday?"

Lange stood back up and ran his eyes over the thick green thorny vines spreading out from the hillside. "No," he said and walked a half dozen steps around Michelle. "I was here." He had both hands out in the air on their sides, marking the edges of his location. He looked up. "And I remember I was staring at all those ripe berries at the base of that fir tree there."

Michelle took two steps right to stand beside him. "You could maybe see his boots from here," she said, assessing the situation. "But these little trees here," she added, touching a three-foot alder that had sprouted at the side of the road, "do a pretty good job of hiding them."

"Mmmmm," Lange reflected.

"And his blue jeans don't jump out, as old as they are." Michelle paced the length of the body, Kojak bumping up against her in his eagerness to work the job. She walked to an opening between some waist-high thistles in the middle of the road, snapped her fingers, and pointed down. Kojak trotted around to where she was pointing and lowered his belly to the ground, his front paws straight out in front of him. "Stay," commanded Michelle.

"He can't have been dead long," said Lange, "because there was no smell yesterday."

"You're sure?"

Lange thought back. He'd been pretty mad when he got here yesterday because of that red Toyota pickup that had sped past him on Sauk Mountain Road. Which made him think. "Maybe he wasn't here when I was here yesterday."

"Somebody dumped him after you left?"

"That's the only way he could have got here, right? His vehicle's not around."

"That's right," agreed Michelle, looking back toward her Range Rover, as if expecting to see another vehicle there.

Lange sighed. The truth was, once he'd gotten into the berries yesterday, he'd stopped paying attention. The only way he could make up for that was to find out what had caused Robert to end up dead in this ditch.

He strode back to the old man's head. "Looks like somebody smacked him hard in the face."

"You think that's what killed him?"

Lange shrugged. "Maybe."

Michelle was teetering over the blackberries to get a closer look. "I'd agree," she said. "Except it looks like there's blood in the dirt by his head, and I don't see blood anywhere on his face."

Lange walked to the other side of the road and picked up a silvery-gray fir limb. He walked back and gently pushed the ferns away from around the old man's head. "Can you see a wound anywhere?"

Michelle craned her neck to see. "There might be a dark stain on the crown of his head, but I'm not—no, I'm not sure."

"Well," said Lange, letting go of the ferns and tossing the stick back to the other side of the road. Kojak watched it go by but didn't move. "We should call it in. Get the sheriff out here so forensics can do their stuff and we can get close enough to the body to figure it out."

"I'll use the radio in my vehicle," said Michelle, but she didn't move from where she was staring down at the dead man.

Lange couldn't bring himself to move, either. "That's a DEA rig, that Range Rover?" he asked, his eyes fixed on the body of Robert Doyle.

"It was seized from a dealer, so we get to use it as an unmarked car. The radio we added, of course."

"Huh. I didn't see a radio."

"It's in the console between the front seats."

Lange nodded.

"What are you thinking?" asked Michelle.

"I just don't get why *this* man, of all people, would be out here waiting for a drug drop."

"Maybe he hit hard times?"

"He *lived* hard times. Why would now be any different?"

"Health issues?"

Lange weighed that in his mind. "I do remember him telling me his wife had something. Alzheimer's, maybe? But I got the impression he'd been coping with that for a while. So why the sudden need to deal drugs?"

"The present administration has been threatening to cut back Medicare coverage . . ."

Lange took his eyes off Robert Doyle and turned them to the woman standing beside him, wondering which side of the political divide this statement put her on. She was petite, maybe five foot four, and as he looked down at her, she lifted her blue eyes to meet his, pushing away from her face a tendril of blonde hair that had escaped from its braid. Lange felt that tug again, then got a grip on himself. What was he thinking?! She was probably half his age. That's when he noticed the challenge in her eyes, as if she were wondering which side of the political divide he stood on, too, and whether he'd blow off her comment as fake news. "That could be it," he said finally. "Desperate times call for desperate measures, kind of thing."

She gave a sharp nod of her head, like she recognized they were on the same page and was glad of it.

"But still," Lange went on, turning back to stare down at the body again. "*Drugs?* I doubt Bob Doyle had ever seen an illegal drug, let alone used one. And now, this late in life—because I think he was in his eighties—he suddenly has connections with someone who wants him to pick up a shipment?"

"Could have been someone he *knew* had the connections. Maybe a kid of his? Or grandkid?"

"Now that's a thought," Lange conceded "He did tell me one of his grandsons was messed up in that somehow." He shook his head vigorously. "No, because it bothered him. A *lot.* So why would he get involved?"

Michelle pushed her pink lips up, contemplating. "What if he came up to *stop* his grandson from making the pickup, and things turned violent?"

Now *that* Lange could picture. "The kid hit his granddad, or pushed him . . ."

". . . which is why all the bruising . . ."

". . . and the blood . . ."

They looked at each other; they were on to something.

"You search the road while I call this in," said Michelle, walking backward, away from Lange. Her leg caught in a sprawling blackberry vine, and it nearly pulled her over.

"Watch out," cautioned Lange. "That's why the locals call these tanglefoot berries."

Michelle spun around and jogged toward the Range Rover.

"What should I do about Kojak?" Lange called after her.

"Have him help."

"Easy for her to say," Lange said to the attentive German shepherd, who was holding the down position. "How am I supposed to make you heel?"

Kojak leapt up and trotted to Lange's left side.

"That was easy," conceded Lange. He took two steps forward, and when Kojak followed suit, Lange walked a long loop, the width of Doyle's body, across the road and back. Kojak stopped where he'd sniffed the road earlier to sniff it again, and Lange crouched down to look for blood. He didn't see any. He took a small piece of rust-brown volcanic rock and placed it where Kojak was sniffing. Then they moved on.

Lange led them slowly back toward the gate, but when they got back to the downed fir tree, the dog leapt over it and instantly became animated, his nose down on the ground, nostrils flaring one, two, three times. Lange stepped over the log and bent forward, peering at the ground. He couldn't see anything of note. "What are you smelling?" he whispered to Kojak.

The dog continued, his nose zigzagging over hardpan and brush toward the uphill side of the road, and when he got to the ditch, he purposely lowered himself to a down, sphinxlike. Lange glanced at the Range Rover and could see Michelle stretching her neck up to see her dog over the dash; something was up.

Lange came alongside Kojak and saw two things: blood and a scrap of folded paper. He fumbled at his hips for a pocket that might be holding something he could use to pick up the paper, then realized he was still in his sweatpants.

"I've got it," shouted Michelle, jogging down the road toward them, flapping a pair of latex gloves for Lange to see. By the time she got to them, she'd snapped them on her fingers in readiness. "What have we found?" she asked, looking down at the ground in front of Kojak. She didn't wait for an answer. Instead she leaned forward and picked up the paper. She held it toward Lange. “That look like blood?” she asked.

“Yep,” he grunted, seeing the reddish-brown thumbprint on one side of the three-by-three scrap.

The paper was folded, and Michelle opened it with her gloved hands. “It’s a check,” she said. “Made out to Kyle Clarkson.”

“The Clarkson brothers,” sighed Lange. “Now why does that not surprise me?”

CHAPTER 3

Michelle reached into the back pocket of her jeans with her thumb and forefinger and teased out an evidence bag. "You know this Clarkson?" she asked, slipping the check into the bag.

"Everyone knows the Clarkson brothers," said Lange. "Well, everyone in the Upper Valley. And probably all of law enforcement down in Mount Vernon. They're the first to be questioned when anything happens up here, usually because they did it. Although," he added, watching Michelle take photos of the blood on the brush. "I thought one of them had settled down. That's what Suleka told me."

"Suleka?"

"My . . ." Lange hesitated. How should he describe Suleka? Most of the time she was the woman who cleaned his yurt, did some of his occasional shopping, drove him to appointments, and kept him updated on local news. But when it came to crime, she was much more than that. "My co-investigator," he said. Then, because he hated to undersell Suleka, he added, "And my friend."

Michelle swung around and met his eye. "Do you think she'd talk to me?"

"Probably," he said. "Although the locals can be tight-lipped with outsiders."

"So make me an insider then."

Lange half smiled. "I'll do my best."

"I'd like to get her take on this Kyle Clarkson before I question him."

"You'll be the one questioning him?" asked Lange, surprised.

"Sure." Michelle's blue eyes had a combative glint in them as she shook the loose hair off her face and pursed her lips. "Why not?"

"You called the Skagit County sheriff to come investigate Robert Doyle's death, correct?"

"Uh-huh."

"Don't you think they'll want to interview Clarkson?"

"About the dead body, yes. I just want to talk to him about the drugs." She motioned for him to come closer. He stepped forward, and she pointed to the ground opposite her dog. "See that?"

Lange saw where the ankle-high grass had been flattened, thistles broken at their bases, like something heavy had sat there. Then his eye caught the white residue on the dark leaves of the blackberries growing out of the ditch. "Good eye!" he exclaimed.

"Good nose," said Michelle, scratching Kojak between the eyes. The dog tipped his head up appreciatively. "The sheriff's office can do all the investigating they want of the body, but any drug charges are mine."

"How can I help?" asked Lange, genuinely awed.

"Can you get me a conversation with your friend?"

"I'll give it a shot." Inwardly he was disappointed. He wanted to be much more active in the investigation of Doyle's death than just making sure people got to talk to each other. In the distance he could hear the sirens floating in and out, like pesky mosquitoes whining around his ear. Somehow they reinforced his impotence in the situation: a retired detective with no ally at the sheriff's office now that Detective Deller was out on maternity leave, and no connections within the local DEA.

"Would you also go talk to Robert Doyle's wife?" said Michelle, as if she'd heard his mental deliberations.

Her request perked Lange up, relieving some of his feelings of uselessness, but he still didn't want to step on any toes. Especially not the toes of local law enforcement.

"Shouldn't I wait for the coroner to get here?"

Michelle was crouched down next to her dog, her face against his muzzle, her hands rubbing vigorously back and forth on the thick fur around his neck, whispering praise for his good work. His question made her stop and look up at him, one eye partly closed against the July sun. "He's dead, Callum, Someone needs to go tell his wife."

Lange nodded; she was right.

"And I cleared it with the sheriff's office already. The detective assigned to this case okayed you to inform the next of kin."

Lange cocked his head. "Which detective?"

"Collins?"

"Collins made it to detective," pondered Lange. "Well, good for him. Okay then," he said, eager to move forward now that he'd been given the go-ahead. "I'll head back down to my yurt, get showered, dress, and then go over to Robert and René's house."

"When will you talk to Suleka?"

"Before I leave, I imagine. She's probably still at my yurt." He threw the statement out casually as he started to walk away, but something about the look on Michelle's face made him rethink the wording. "Cleaning it," he called out. "She comes to clean for me twice a month."

Michelle's brow cleared and she jumped up, brushing dog hair off her jeans. She flicked her hand at Kojak, a nonverbal command for him to maintain his down. "The Range Rover's unlocked," she shouted after Lange. "I have some business cards in the cup holder between the seats. Why don't you reach inside and get one, so you can call me later for updates."

The ex-detective threw a thumb up into the air and stretched out toward the end of the road, feeling pretty darn good. He slipped back around the heavy yellow gate, ducking under a slender, overhanging wild cherry tree, and pulled open the door of the Rover. He loosened one of Michelle's business cards, tucked it into the palm of his hand, and continued the jaunt down the road toward his property.

His mind lingered on the way Michelle had used his name—"He's dead, Callum"—like they'd known each other a long time. And how, when she'd confronted him about why she shouldn't be the one to question Clarkson, the hint of teal in her blue eyes had reminded him of Ross Lake on a cloudless summer day. He was already enjoying being part of this investigation. Maybe that's what his ex-partner was alluding to when he said, "the comfort of your presence."

Jimmy had come out for a short visit back in May, and while he and Lange sat drinking scotch and watching the sunset from lawn chairs on the ridge overlooking the Skagit River, the young New Yorker had seemed restless with their total seclusion. "Don't you get lonely?" he asked.

"You forget I don't like people that much," Lange replied.

"You don't like assholes," Jimmy remarked. "I get that." He took a slug of his whiskey, then looked at Lange. "But there's people out there that can put a real lift in your day."

Lange didn't say anything, even though part of him agreed. He certainly got a lift from the fact that this kid had chosen to spend his few vacation days out in the Skagit with him.

"I mean, I don't know about you," said Jimmy, "but I miss the way we bounced ideas off each other when we were partners."

"Sure," said Lange, skipping the fact that he did the same thing with Suleka now. "But we can still do that long distance."

That was when Jimmy said, "We can. But I don't get the comfort of your presence that way."

Lange had found himself thinking about that phrase ever since.

He heard the sirens circling up Sauk Mountain Road as he walked through the gate at the end of his long driveway. He was glad he hadn't encountered any of the vehicles. He almost jogged the last few hundred yards toward his thirty-foot-diameter brown canvas yurt, wanting to get back out on the road again so he'd be available when the preliminary forensics came in.

Suleka's Nissan pickup was still there. Good. He'd ask her to drive him over to René Doyle's. He bounded up the steps to his tiny deck and tugged off his sneakers, then stopped, his hand on the door. Was that a whine? He waited, thinking he might hear it again, but there was nothing.

He stepped in to find Suleka finishing up his dishes. "Well, don't you look happy," she burst out at him, her eyes piercing through his composure like she might uncover the reason behind it.

"Is it because we've got another case?"

"How'd you know that?!"

She gave him a scathing look. "I heard the sirens, of course. I figured they were either coming to arrest you or to get your help. Where's your Prius by the way?"

"I lent it to José. You know, the guy that's going to start milling some of my logs?" he replied, placing Michelle's card down on his writing desk before walking over the Scrabble game. He looked at the board and felt his mouth fall open.

"Yes, I know José. Good. I was worried when I didn't see it parked at the bottom of the road." She peered across at his desk, then followed her curiosity and went to pick up the card. "Ahhh, now I get it."

"Get what?" Lange muttered, still staring down at the Scrabble board. He thought he'd stumped her playing *quested* yesterday, but apparently not.

"The reason for your good humor." She held up the card and read. "Michelle Pate-Swenson. Is she cute?"

Lange's head shot up. "What?"

"Come on, don't deny it," Suleka goaded. "You're blushing."

"I'm sixty-one years old," argued Lange. "I don't blush."

"New love's still new love no matter how old you are."

"Oh stop," he rebuked, but not very forcefully. "As a matter of fact, it's you she wants to talk to." He snatched a towel off the chair beside his bed.

"Me?" protested Suleka, her voice so high it rang like a bell in the circle of the yurt. "I don't do drugs."

"What's that got to do with anything?"

She held up the card. "It says DEA."

Lange laughed. "She just wants to pick your brain about some of the locals."

"Which ones?"

"The Clarkson brothers."

"Oh. Why? What have they done?"

"She doesn't know. That's why she wants to talk to you."

"But why all the emergency vehicles?"

Lange headed for the door, ready for the conversation to be over. "I'll tell you about it in the car."

"We're leaving *now*?"

"After I shower."

Suleka placed the card back on the desk. "Yep," she declared. "She's cute."

CHAPTER 4

Lange buckled up next to Suleka as she started the vehicle. The Nissan was so old it didn't have a cup holder in the front, but she had hung one from the air vent on the dash and Lange used it for his coffee. He rolled his window down to release some of the stuffiness that had permeated the vehicle while it sat out in the sun, and thought he heard that whining sound again. He poked his head out to listen.

"What're you doing?"

"Did you hear something?"

"Like what?"

"No, it's nothing," said Lange, pulling his head back in. He peeled the lid off the plastic container on his lap and dug his fork into a chunk of salmon quiche. He tossed the quiche into his mouth and chomped down on it. He hadn't eaten since a few apple chips early in the morning, when he was writing, and his stomach ached with hunger.

"Where're we going?"

Lange swallowed. "Robert and René Doyle's house. D'you know where that is?"

"Uh-huh. Why're we going there?"

"I have to tell René that Robert's dead."

"Ohhhh," lamented Suleka. "Robert Doyle's dead. That's too bad. But he was getting up there . . . Hang on a minute," she said, her tone sharper. She flipped her long silvery-brown braid over her shoulder. "Why do *you* have to tell her? What happened to him? Is he something to do with all these emergency vehicles?"

Lange nodded, his mouth full.

"What? Somebody killed him? Sweet, harmless Robert Doyle?! That's terrible."

She turned right at the end of the driveway, hammering the

Nissan down Sauk Mountain Road. Lange went to wash down his quiche with coffee so he could answer her and nearly spilled the lot all over himself. "Woah!" he shouted. "Slow down."

Suleka slowed to a stop at the side of the road, and Callum looked up, surprised that she'd done what he asked so completely. Then he saw the dark-brown Chevy Suburban coming toward them. He drank quickly while the Nissan wasn't moving, the coffee burning the sides of his mouth. "We don't know for sure that Doyle was killed yet," he said. "But it looks that way. And we think it had something to do with his grandson."

"We?"

"Me and the DEA agent, Pate-Swenson."

"What does she know about Robert Doyle's grandson?" scoffed Suleka.

A cheerful young woman smiled and waved at them as she drove past.

"Good deal!" remarked Lange.

"What?" said Suleka.

"The coroner got the four-wheel-drive vehicle she's been lobbying for," he explained, waving back at Shelley Tomeoka.

"Kevin's not very smart when it comes to girlfriends," said Suleka, pulling back out now that the Suburban had gone by and driving slower than before. "But he would never kill his grandfather. Why would you even think that?"

Lange leaned forward and slipped his coffee back into the makeshift cup holder. "We don't. Not exactly. It's like a puzzle where the pieces don't seem to want to fit together."

"Give me some of the pieces. Maybe I'll have better luck."

"Okay. A shipment of drugs up on Sauk. That's how come Pate-Swenson was up there."

"A shipment of *drugs*?"

"I know. That's what I said. But apparently this is a great area for covert dumping of drugs out of small planes."

"Ohhhh, you know I've heard about that."

"You have?"

"Yes. Not planes but helicopters. I've heard there's a meadow on North Mountain where the debris field—you know, the twigs and sticks and bark and leaves—is entirely on the perimeter because the rotors on the helicopters blow it there when they land to deliver the drugs."

Lange was surprised. "How come you never told me that?"

"You never asked."

"Hmmm." He put another piece of quiche in his mouth.

Suleka reached the bottom of Sauk Mountain Road and turned right onto Highway 20. "Give me some more puzzle pieces."

"Robert Doyle's dead body. And a check made out to Kyle Clarkson."

"A check made out to Kyle Clarkson?"

"Yes. And it had blood on it."

"Oh, this is not good. This is not *good*!" cried Suleka. "Kyle Clarkson has been real steady ever since his daughter, Alice, was born."

"I remember you telling me something like that."

"I'd hate to see him go back to his old ways. When is this all supposed to have happened?"

"Yesterday. Maybe early morning."

"Kyle works at the mill in Darrington, so it should be easy enough to find out if he was working yesterday."

"Good to know."

"And what about Kevin? Was there some kind of incriminating evidence of him being up there, too?"

"No. But it's the only logical explanation for why his grandfather was up there."

"To try to stop him from getting involved in drugs again. I see that." Suleka became agitated. "But I still don't see him killing his grandfather. If they'd been up there at the same time and somebody had gone for Robert Doyle, I see Kevin trying to protect him, not just let it happen."

Lange sighed. "And maybe he'll tell us that when we get the chance to talk to him. Maybe it was all just one big accident. But if that was the case, I don't see why Bob Doyle's body is still lying in a ditch up on Sauk."

He forked himself another chunk of quiche and threw it into his mouth. His eyes bounced over the sunlit surface of the Skagit River as the Nissan trundled past Faber Landing and headed for the bend in the road leading to Faber Hill.

"We'll probably see Kevin with his grandmother, and I'm sure—*I'm sure*—he'll make sense of what happened for us. I've known Kevin most of his life, and yes, he's been known to hang out with the Clarksons, but he's always been very responsible when it comes to his family, even though he can't seem to make it work to live with the mother of his children for more than a couple of months at a time. Of course, I've heard she's in and out of rehab, so it's not all his fault . . ."

Lange let her chatter on as they sailed down the hill. He munched more sedately on the quiche, noticing how good it was now that he had time to actually enjoy it rather than just inhale it, and he contemplated Robert Doyle's absence from home. Why hadn't René said anything to anyone? Or had she? Did she even live at their home anymore? Maybe she was in a care center because of her Alzheimer's. He hadn't known Doyle that well, but he was pretty sure the old fellow had been a creature of habit. Why hadn't anyone called the sheriff saying he hadn't come home? Or had they?

They drove past the wood-carver's place and around to the short stretch of road where the steep uphill often slid down toward the river during the rainy season, covering the highway in saturated mud, rocks, and broken saplings. Lange took the last bite of his quiche, looking at the proliferation of summer greens on the hillside. It looked pretty settled right now, he thought.

They crossed the Baker River and turned into Robert Doyle's driveway. "See, Kevin's truck is here," Suleka remarked, pointing ahead of them at a beat-up Ford Ranger. "He's probably inside making lunch for his grandmother like I told you."

Lange snapped the lid back on the plastic container the quiche had come in and placed it on the floor by his feet. "It was good," he said.

"The quiche? I'm glad you liked it." She glared at him as he unbuckled his seat belt. "Did you hear *anything* I said to you?"

"What?"

Suleka tsked her irritation, but Lange was already out the door and striding toward the small, dilapidated wood-frame cottage. He got to the front door and went to rap on it, but it swung open before he could make contact. A wiry young man, who smelled like he'd just walked through a cluster of Christmas trees, stood facing Lange, pale chips of sawdust on his jeans and t-shirt, in his dark curls and moustache, giving a reason for the smell. The youth's feet shifted, like he wasn't sure about this, but he made direct eye contact. Guarded but not evasive, thought Lange.

"Yep?"

"Kevin, how are you?" Suleka called out on her way to the front door.

"Hey, Suleka, what's up?" Kevin replied.

Lange stepped to one side to allow Suleka the lead since Kevin obviously seemed at ease with her.

"Is your grandmother home?" she asked. "We need to talk to her."

"Yeah, she's here. Come on in."

Suleka stepped through the doorway and into a boxy living room, ahead of Kevin, then Lange. There were two overstuffed armchairs and a battered couch crowding the room, with an old-style TV directly opposite where they came in. René Doyle was sitting in the armchair closest to the door, her back to them, watching some kind of soap opera.

Suleka edged around the side of the armchair, her face tipped down. "Hi, René," she said. She dropped her hand to touch the old lady's. "How are you?"

"Kevin, someone's here," René called out. She didn't sound scared, just surprised.

Kevin squeezed past Suleka and put himself in front of his grandmother. Suleka swung around and crouched on the other side of René, holding her left hand now, which gave Lange enough space to come into the tiny room, where René could see him.

The old woman's dark eyes clouded at the unusual presence in the room. She looked confused, panicked. "Kevin?" she uttered.

"It's okay, Grandma. These people have just come to see you. You remember Suleka? And this is . . ."

"Callum Lange. I'm sorry I didn't get a chance to tell you that earlier."

"S'okay."

René's eyes cleared and she smiled at Suleka. "I remember you! You helped my Bob do exercises after he broke his leg. Did you see him walking around outside? Looks good, don't he?"

"He's not there, René," Suleka said gently. "That's what we came to talk to you about."

"He is there," argued René. "Ask Kevin. He told me they was just cutting up some fir together. Didn't you, Kev?"

And suddenly Kevin Doyle didn't look so comfortable anymore.

CHAPTER 5

"What's happened?" the young man asked after he recovered his composure, his eyes shifting from Lange to Suleka and back again. "Where's my grandpa?"

"I'm sorry to say we found him dead up on Sauk Mountain," Lange told him.

Kevin Doyle buckled like he'd been punched in the stomach.

"Who's up on Sauk Mountain?" René asked, curious.

"Your husband, Bob," Suleka told her gently, stroking the old woman's hand.

"Bob's not up on Sauk!" argued René. "He's with Kevin."

"He's not, Grandma. I'm right here," said Kevin, pulling himself back to a stand. There was compassion in his tone, like he was preparing for the role he knew he must take on, of telling her the worst. He sucked in a deep breath and faced Lange again. "What'd he die of?"

"We're not sure," said Lange. "We found him in a ditch on an abandoned logging road. It looks like someone hit him."

Kevin's mouth gaped open. "So you're saying . . . What are you saying?" he stammered, looking from one to the other of them again. Lange got the impression he was genuinely surprised. "You're saying, like, he didn't die of a heart attack or something?"

"Who's dead?" asked René.

"Not by the looks of it, no."

Kevin slumped down onto the arm of the chair opposite René, his eyes shifting left and right, as if he was trying to come to grips with what he'd just heard.

Lange pressed on. "And we need to ask you where you were yesterday."

"What?" said Kevin, like he hadn't heard. Then the question registered. "At my girlfriend's."

"I hope you're not with that Cheryl again," René put in. "Grandpa said he was going to talk to you about that."

"Cheryl who?" asked Lange.

"Grandma . . ."

"Was that where you saw Grandpa?" she asked. "At Cheryl's house."

"No, I told you," insisted Kevin to his grandmother. "I haven't seen Grandpa Bob since the day before yesterday." He put his face in his hands, hiding his frustration and, Lange guessed, his sorrow.

"And where was Robert when you last saw him?" persisted the ex-detective.

"Robert?" asked René. "Robert's outside. I was hungry and he said he was going outside to look for Kevin." She paused, then asked her grandson, "Is it lunchtime?"

Kevin shook his head despondently without lifting it out of his hands. "You had your lunch already, Grandma."

"Well, Grandpa's going to talk to you about those boys you've been hanging out with. They're not good boys."

"Which boys would those be?" asked Lange of Kevin.

Now Kevin thrust his head up, shedding sawdust from his hair onto the armchair. "How should I know?" he argued. "She could be talking about some kids I went to grade school with for all I know." He held his hand out, palm up, toward his grandmother. "You see how she is."

Suleka threw Lange an anguished look; it was true.

"Where's Grandpa's body now?!" Kevin snapped, bitterness masking the pain in his deep-brown eyes.

"Whose body?" asked René.

"He was *my* grandfather. I have a right to know."

The room was filling up with pain.

"I don't know," admitted Lange. "The coroner was on her way up to get the body when we came down to talk to you. Eventually she'll take him to the morgue at the hospital in Mount Vernon, for an autopsy."

Kevin's face crumpled, like he wanted to cry.

"Whose body??" insisted René.

Suleka rose and touched Kevin's shoulder in kindness, but he shrugged her off. He stood upright again and blinked hard, looking away from Lange as if hiding tears.

"I'm sorry for your loss," said the retired detective. He felt awkward, standing in a room where he knew he was superfluous.

The old woman edged forward in her chair, her arms stretched toward her grandson. "What's the matter, honey?" she said. "Who's dead?"

Kevin knelt in front of her chair and took both her hands in his. "Grandma, I need to tell you something."

Lange nodded for Suleka to follow him. "We'll be back in touch," he said.

"Yeah, right," groaned Kevin. "Hey, wait," he said as Lange opened the front door. "Where's Max?"

Now Lange was confused.

"My grandpa's dog?" explained Kevin.

"Max is outside with Grandpa," answered René. "I thought you guys were working on cutting up that fir log. Isn't that what you told me?"

"Wait a minute, Grandma," Kevin whispered to René.

Suleka was shaking her head. "We didn't see a dog up there."

"I'm sure he must have been with Grandpa, 'cause he's not here. Can I go up and look for him?"

His manner was eager, maybe too eager, Lange thought, given his grief. Suspicion began to edge out his compassion for this young man.

"Not until the crime scene investigators have finished up on Sauk," he said.

Kevin sat back on his heels, a faraway look in his eyes. "Crime scene," he repeated, anguished by the words.

Lange knew he wouldn't be able to clarify further, so he exited quickly and hurried over to the Nissan. But once he was inside the vehicle, the pressure to be on his way seemed to dissipate. "Maybe I'm out of practice," he admitted to Suleka as she climbed in beside him.

"Practice of what?"

"Informing the next of kin." He shook his head, irritated with himself, as he stared out the open passenger window at the tiny cottage with its peeling paint and mossy asphalt roof. "I botched that whole thing. Starting with not knowing how to tell someone with René Doyle's affliction that her husband is dead." He spun to face Suleka, searching for answers. "How do you do that? Tell someone who doesn't necessarily know who their husband is that he's dead?"

A long, pained howl rose from the weathered cabin and shattered the quiet inside the Nissan.

"That's how," murmured Suleka.

Lange felt the howl penetrate every pore on his body and suffuse his core, where it stirred compassion and pain and a need to help. "You were right when you said Kevin's close to his grandparents."

Suleka started the Nissan, backed it around into a well-rutted mud alleyway alongside the cottage, then pulled forward up the driveway. "You *were* listening," she said.

"Some," Lange admitted. "He seemed genuinely distraught about Bob's death."

"I told you he wasn't the kind of kid that would kill his grandfather."

"I believe that now. But I am wondering if he was distraught simply because Robert was dead or because he was somehow involved with the Clarksons? He's got to know that if he was, he sent his grandfather to his doom."

"Yet he looked so surprised when you said 'crime scene.'"

"True," said Lange, thinking about her answer. "But again that could be because he's rationalized that what happened to his grandfather wasn't a crime."

"I didn't get the impression that he even knew what had

happened to his grandfather," countered Suleka. She shrugged. "But, you know, I'm not the detective here."

They were sitting at the end of Doyle's driveway, and Lange looked up at the top of Sauk, with its patches of snow laced like winter spiderwebs over the bright emerald green of the high meadows.

"Which way?" asked Suleka.

"What?"

"Which way are we going from here?"

Lange paused. "I'm not really sure. We could go back up Sauk and see what the coroner determined about the body, but I don't want to be just another pair of boots trampling potential evidence on that brushy road." He thought for a moment, watching the traffic crawl by in the thirty-five-miles-per-hour zone that was Concrete. "I'd go and talk to one of the Clarkson brothers—or both—but it might be too early for that. I don't want to botch that, too." He thought some more. "I guess if we went back up Sauk, you could talk to Pate-Swenson about the Clarksons."

"Why does she want to talk to me about them again?"

"Because didn't you tell me one of them had straightened up his act?"

"Well, that's what I heard. Ever since he became a daddy, he's been towing the line."

"See, and that's information that would be helpful to Pate-Swenson."

"Except that's about the extent of what I know."

"Hmmm. And I don't know if she's ready for us yet. She might be knee-deep in forensics."

"Can't you call her?"

He sat up, energized, and slapped at his shirt pockets. "I can! Where did I put her business card?"

"On your desk. In your yurt."

"Damn!"

"We could go back up and get it."

Lange said nothing. He sat, staring ahead, seeing the faraway look in Kevin Doyle's eyes.

"Look, if we're not in a hurry to go anywhere, why don't we go to the grocery store? If we're lucky, Jen will be working one of the cash registers, and I can leave you to talk to her while I do your shopping. Your fridge is a pretty sorry state right now. You're lucky I brought you that quiche."

"Why would I want to talk to this Jen?"

"Because one of her daughters is who married Kyle Clarkson. They're not married anymore but they have a daughter together."

"Oh, good thinking," said Lange, his interest rising. "Though we'd better not say anything about what's happened yet."

Suleka pulled out of the driveway, turning left onto the highway. "I know that," she said, her tone aggrieved.

"I know you do," Lange assured her. "It's just going to be awkward saying this investigator wants to talk to her without telling her why."

"I'm sure we'll come up with something."

"Yes. I'm sure we will." Lange looked across at her, wanting to make up for any offense he may have given. "I do feel lucky that you brought me that quiche, and not just because it was extra tasty."

Suleka made a conciliatory pout. "Okay, you're forgiven."

"Which one is Jen?" Lange asked.

"She's the short one with the dark hair in a tidy kind of sweep that curls around her ears back onto her face. Like a mini bob cut. You know what I mean?"

"Not really."

"Okay, well . . ." Suleka thought about how best to describe the cashier as she picked up speed leaving the city limits. "She has big brown eyes and full Cupid's bow lips."

"Does she walk with a limp?"

"I think she does, yes." She cocked her head, trying to imagine it. "Maybe sometimes."

"And she's not very tall?"

"I said she was short."

"Oh," conceded Lange. "Then yes, I think I know the one you mean."

"That's her there," said Suleka as she pulled into the Albert's parking lot. "Just walking out of the store. You might be in luck."

"How so?"

"It looks like she's on break."

The clerk continued walking away from the door until she reached a red metal barrier by some soda machines. She leaned on the barrier, looking across at the pizza parlor opposite, and lit a cigarette.

"You know that's bad for you, right?" teased Suleka as she and Lange walked toward the clerk.

Jen swung around to face them, tucking herself back in against the metal. "Yeah. But I've got to have at least one vice, and I gave up men and alcohol."

"That's funny, I gave up men, too," admitted Suleka. "But not alcohol. I'll drink, you smoke, and we'll call it even, huh?"

The clerk laughed, stuffing her free hand down inside the front pouch of her red work apron as she took a long drag on her cigarette.

"My friend here was hoping you might have a moment for him," Suleka added, her left hand out to indicate Lange.

"Me?" said the woman, turning her head toward the pizza parlor to exhale the smoke from her cigarette, so it wouldn't blow in their faces.

"I have a couple of questions if you don't mind," explained Lange.

"You're the detective, right?" said Jen.

"Retired detective, but yes, you might have heard about me that way."

"Does this have anything to do with all the emergency vehicles that went screaming past here an hour or so ago? I heard something happened up on Sauk."

Suleka lifted her eyebrows to Lange; so much for keeping it

quiet.

Jen pushed herself off the metal barrier, looking alarmed. "Oh no, it's not one of my kids, is it?"

"No, no, nothing like that," Lange reassured her. "I'm Callum Lange," he said to introduce himself, "and I need a little information about Kyle Clarkson. Suleka told me you might be able to help me."

"What's he done now?" said Jen, like she'd been expecting this.

Suleka interrupted them, pointing toward the store. "If you don't mind, I'm going to leave you and go shop."

"Please," said Jen, flapping her hand to suggest she should go.

"We don't know that he's done anything," Lange answered the store clerk. "I'm just trying to find out a little bit more about him, and Suleka indicated you might be the person to talk to."

"Okay," said Jen and took another drag on her cigarette before going on. "What d'you want to know?"

"Whether you think he's still on the straight and narrow?"

Jen blew her cigarette smoke up into the air above her head. "Last I knew," she said. "He's waaaay different than he was when he met my daughter, if that's what you mean. Not that I wasn't disappointed when she chose to marry him." She looked off into the distance and shook her head slightly. "He had a terrible reputation. Just terrible! But my daughter's got a good head on her shoulders—well, all three of them do."

"You have three daughters?"

"Uh-huh. Triplets," she added.

"Oh my word."

"That's what I said when they came out. Well," she corrected. "I guess I said something not nearly that polite!" And she laughed, a deep, throaty laugh, her brown eyes lit up with merriment. "But they're my pride and joy. And I have to say, my daughter Brandie was exactly what Kyle Clarkson needed. He settled right down. Especially when little Alice was born. He only screwed up once, led by that brother of his, and Brandie divorced him over it. He said he'd never do it again, and she said he sure wouldn't if she divorced him.

She's still friends with him. Says she always will be. But she didn't want to be an enabler, that's what she told me." She took another puff of her cigarette and turned her head again to exhale. When she looked back at Lange, she had a pensive look in her eyes. "I didn't think Kyle would screw up again after that. Not with how much he loves Alice. He even helps homeschool her."

"How old is Alice?"

"She's eight. And the sweetest little eight-year-old you'd ever want to meet." She said the words happily, her shoulders rocking slightly with the joy of it. She positioned her cigarette close to her mouth, ready to take another drag, and her face became more serious, her eyes harder. "What happened up on Sauk?"

"Do you know if Kyle hangs around with Kevin Doyle at all?"

"Kevin?" she asked, holding the smoke in her lungs. "Bob and René's grandson?" She exhaled toward the pizza parlor. "I don't think so. They used to, but then Kyle married my Brandie and she said that Kevin wasn't the good kind of friend and Kyle agreed. So he stopped hanging out with him. Plus Kevin settled down himself once he had a kid with his girlfriend." She thought about this for a moment. "Maybe two, I can't remember. It's been a while since I've seen Kevin."

"And Brandie hasn't said anything to you about things not being usual yesterday?"

"You know, she did, now that I think about it. I'm glad you said that. We had coffee together this morning—I always stop by her house on Tuesday mornings for coffee—Tuesdays and Thursdays. And I stop at the other girls' houses Monday and Friday and Wednesday and Saturday. Sunday we all sleep in, even if I have to work, because the store opens later on Sunday. Anyway, I stopped by Brandie's today, and Alice didn't want to come out of her bedroom. She usually eats her breakfast next to me while I drink my coffee and visit with Brandie, but today she had her head in a book. Which isn't bad, but when I asked Brandie about it, she said she'd come back from spending the day with Kyle real quiet. Like something was up that she didn't want to talk about." She took another drag on her cigarette and looked up, thinking.

A motorbike roared into the parking lot, and Lange heard part of a conversation about renting a movie from some people coming up behind him on their way into the store. The doors swished open, and the general noise of the business floated out toward him as he waited for Jen to go on.

She tapped the air with the hand holding the cigarette, remembering. "And I guess Alice was supposed to go someplace with Kyle yesterday." She thought some more. "The fish hatchery, that was it. A kind of field trip, like in school. But when Brandie asked her about it, Alice said they didn't go because of Uncle Wayne."

Lange zeroed in on this point. "So Uncle Wayne *is* allowed to hang out with Kyle."

"Well, Brandie couldn't stop that relationship, because Wayne's his brother, of course. And Alice's uncle. Kyle's just not supposed to get involved in any of Wayne's criminal activities."

"Do you know what Alice meant by 'because of Uncle Wayne'?"

"I don't, no," she replied, dropping the end of her cigarette on the ground and stepping on it. She exhaled the last of the smoke, picked up the butt, and slipped it back in the box. "Brandie couldn't get her to say. And she didn't want to push it, so she said she was going to ask Kyle today."

"He didn't mention anything yesterday?"

"No, because he didn't get out of his truck when he brought Alice back."

"Is that usual?"

"I'm not sure. I mean, I'm not there so . . ." She held her hands up in the air, like it was anyone's guess.

"No, I get it."

"But Brandie sometimes tells me about the stories they share when they trade off Alice on a school day." She made air quotation marks when she said 'school.' "You know, the things she did good at, the things she struggled with. So I guess he usually stops. But he's working swing shift at the mill in Darrington these days, and Brandie did say he was cutting it kind of fine to get to work on time yesterday, so he didn't even look at her when Alice got out of his pickup."

"Do you think she'd mind if I went and asked her a few questions?"

"Probably not. Especially if Kyle's been up to something. She'd want to know that for sure."

"And she's home today?"

"Yep. Today's one of her days home with Alice." She pulled her phone out of her apron pocket and glanced at it. "I have just enough time to call her if you like. Tell her you're going to stop by."

Lange wavered. "I have to check with the detective overseeing the case first. He may or may not want me to talk to your daughter." He held his hand out toward her. "Although feel free to call her; see if she's willing to talk to me if I get the go-ahead." Then he leaned in a little closer, his tone more confidential. "But I'd prefer others didn't know that I have some questions for her."

Jen slipped her phone back in the pouch of her apron. "I get it. It's like me not wanting to know the Seahawks score when I'm working during one of their games. Don't. Say. A word!"

"I'd appreciate that."

They walked side by side the few steps back toward the doors, which swished apart to let them in; then they moved as if they'd entered independently of one another. Jen hustled over to her cash register while Lange stopped by the magazine rack. He looked out toward the aisles, searching for Suleka. He saw her over by the coffee beans and could hear the whirr of the grinding machine. She had her back to Lange and was talking to a woman he didn't recognize. He felt his phone vibrate in his pocket and pulled it out to see that he'd missed a call from a blocked ID. There was no voice mail. He'd been hoping for a call from Collins; maybe that had been it, he thought. But then again, he wasn't sure he had the kind of rapport with Deputy—no, *Detective*—Collins, he corrected himself, to prompt him to call with updates. He pushed the phone back into his pocket and looked up to see Suleka had moved. She was at Jen's register, unloading groceries onto the short moving belt. Lange walked across to join her.

"How'd it go?" Suleka asked the two of them, dropping a half dozen pots of yogurt on the conveyor.

"How'd what go?" replied Jen. She grinned at Lange, pleased with herself to have kept his secret.

"Attagirl," he acknowledged with a return grin.

But he filled Suleka in on their conversation when they walked across the parking lot with the two bags of groceries she'd had him purchase.

She listened attentively, then said, "I think I may know why Kyle was reluctant to talk to Brandie yesterday."

"Why?"

"I got chatting with my friend Eve over by the coffee grinder," she said, looking both sides of her, not wanting to be overheard.

Lange motioned for them to get in the truck. It was stuffy in the Nissan with the windows rolled up, but quiet. And private.

"Eve used to be Kyle's boss," Suleka continued once they were sitting side by side. "So, you know, I asked her how she was? How was work? She told me pretty good. She's getting close to retirement. So I said, 'How's Kyle doing?' 'Kyle Clarkson?' she said. 'I think okay. He's not working my shift anymore. I'm on days and he works swing shift.'"

"Which would have made him free to be up on Sauk yesterday, I know," interjected Lange. "Jen told me about the swing shift. But she also said he was with Alice."

"Oh. Well, Alice is old enough to be left alone for a while, I would think."

"Maybe."

"Well, anyway, Eve went on to say, 'If he's still got a job.'"

"What did she mean by that?"

"Give me a minute. I'm getting there," remonstrated Suleka. She leaned forward, an excited look on her face. "She said he turned up at work ten minutes late yesterday—she noticed because she was on her way out and he usually arrives before her shift is over—and he had a big, old, fat lip and an angry-looking cut on one side of his temple. Plus he was in the kind of mood that made her want to keep her distance."

Lange let his head bob up and down as he pondered what she'd told him. "Was he now," he said.

"Okay, where to?" Suleka asked, straightening up in her seat and turning on the engine. "I'm thinking we should take the groceries back to your yurt," she went on, answering her own question. "And while I put them away, you can call your friend Michelle. Find out where you need to go next."

"She's not my friend," corrected Lange, understanding exactly what Suleka meant by that word. "She's a DEA agent that I only met today, but yes, that's a good idea. I might also make a pot of coffee. I could use a cup and she probably could, too. It might be a while before they get forensics finished up there. What time is it?" he asked and then looked at his own watch for the answer. "It's almost one thirty already. Maybe I should make her some lunch while I'm at it. What do you think?"

They were at the exit of the parking lot, waiting to pull out onto the highway. Suleka graced Lange with an enigmatic smile.

"What?"

"She's *not* your friend?"

"Oh stop," he insisted. Then added, so she would know and not keep on with her teasing, "She's too young to be that kind of friend to me."

"How d'you know? Did you ask her age?"

"No-o!" exclaimed Lange.

"Well, there you go then." Suleka pulled out onto the highway and headed back in the direction of Sauk. "I'm sure she'd appreciate you making her some lunch, though. And you can do that because I got you bread and sandwich meat."

The mention of bread jogged a memory in Lange. A memory of leaning into Michelle's Range Rover to get her business card and seeing a bag of some kind of snack food on the passenger seat. What was it he'd noticed about the bag? "Gluten-free," he blurted, his index finger in the air.

"What?"

"No, I was just thinking, Michelle may not prefer a sandwich. She might not eat gluten."

They were approaching the thirty-five-miles-per-hour zone through Concrete again. "Well, let's stop at 5b's Bakery," said Suleka. "They have some great gluten-free lunch items."

"But what if I'm wrong?" he asked, worried about imposing something on Michelle that she might not prefer.

"Then you can eat it for lunch tomorrow."

"Why would I do that?" asked Lange. "I eat gluten."

"Doesn't matter. You like 5b's food."

"I do?"

They were heading up Superior Avenue toward Main Street in Concrete. "Well, you loved that bumbleberry pie I bought you last week."

"Oh," muttered Lange, looking at all the handmade birdhouses on the fence of the community garden as they drove by. "I didn't know that was gluten-free."

"See, life can still surprise you."

They pulled them into the narrow gravel parking lot alongside the bakery, and Suleka switched off the engine.

"Let's do this quick," said Lange. "I want to get back up the mountain and relate what we've found out. Good work, by the way."

They hurried past the people seated at outside tables, admiring the view of Sauk, and went into the bakery. The space was very inviting, with a long, knotty fir table at waist height dividing the seating area and two counters, one with a glass display of fresh baked items and one with an old-fashioned soda fountain, ahead of them and to their left. The windows to their right all boasted a perfect view of Sauk, and there were shelf units with local art, notecards, and books for people to peruse while they waited for whatever gluten-free treat they had in mind. Many of the tables were occupied, but the display counter had only one person at the register, paying for their items.

"See, these are all the savories," said Suleka, bringing Lange to the display closest to the register. "And the sweet treats are there," she added, pointing across him to their right. "You can get a sandwich made on their gluten-free bread or buy one of these prebaked calzones or an egg mini stratta."

"What's that?"

She pointed at the muffin-sized concoctions below in the display. "They're like a popover made with eggs. Some have bacon and cheese in them, some sausage and pepper. And look, there's some with just sun-dried tomatoes and Asiago cheese."

"Maybe we'll get one of each of those. Like you said, what she doesn't eat, I can."

"Perfect."

"Do you want one?"

"I am kind of hungry. I was thinking I'd eat some of my quiche when I got home, but I guess I'm not going home for a while."

"I'll buy you what you want."

"Well, in that case . . ."

They walked out of the bakery with three egg mini stratta, a calzone, a bagel dog, a cinnamon roll, a peanut-butter bar, and two bumbleberry pies.

"Busy place," remarked Lange as Suleka drove them back out to the highway.

He glanced at the Doyle house on their way by and started mentally replaying the conversation with René and Kevin Doyle. It wasn't until they were most of the way up Sauk Mountain that he reheard the last thing Kevin said to him and instantly made the connection.

As soon as Suleka pulled up at the end of his driveway, in front of his yurt, he leapt out of the Nissan, clutching the bag of goodies from 5b's.

"Where are you . . . ?" Suleka called out.

But Lange wasn't paying attention. He was creeping counterclockwise around the yurt, his body bent at the waist, the bag from 5b's pushed up against his chest, peering through the cedar lattice around the crawl space. He was hoping to hear that whining sound again. But if he didn't hear the sound, maybe he could track down what was behind it.

He circled the entire yurt, and when he reached the small porch built in front of his door, he stopped, straightening to a stand again. Suleka had just reached the steps, carrying a bag of groceries from the back of the Nissan, and she stopped, watching him. "What are you—?" she started again.

"Shush!" Lange interrupted. He pulled one arm free from clutching the baked goods and cupped his ear with it: *listen*!

There was nothing. Then they both heard it at the same time: the faint sound of an animal in distress, coming from under the porch. Lange eased closer to the space, crouched down on his haunches, and peered into the shadowy area. He saw the pair of startled eyes peering back at him. "Hi there," he whispered. "You must be Max."

CHAPTER 6

Suleka gasped. "Is that Bob's dog?"

"That would be my assumption." Lange set the bag of baked goods down and stretched his right hand forward, palm down. "Come on out, little buddy. Are you hungry?"

The whining increased, then Lange felt a wet nose sniffing his fingers. The dog must have satisfied himself that he was safe, because he slunk forward and emerged, head down, his tail flickering from side to side even though it was down, too.

"Hey, you're okay. You're okay now," Lange crooned to the terrified pup as he gently stroked his back. The Jack Russell pushed a little closer to Lange but still kept his head down.

"That's Bob's dog alright," said Suleka, holding her position at the bottom of the steps. "He looks like he's hurt."

"I see that," said Lange, having spotted the ugly red tear in Max's otherwise white fur, up by his right shoulder. "It doesn't look too deep but he's obviously been worrying it. "Come on," he said to the pup, "let's get that cleaned up and get you something to eat and drink."

Suleka headed inside the yurt and came back out a few moments later with a sliver of ham to tease the dog up the steps.

"Thanks," said Lange, who'd been struggling to convince Max to come inside.

"You go ahead and make your call," Suleka said. "And I'll get the coffee water started and clean up the dog's wound."

It was warm inside the yurt from the sun heating the canvas walls and pouring in through the skylight above his desk, but Lange didn't want Max to escape before Suleka had a chance to look at his wound, so he deposited the bag from 5b's on the counter in his kitchen and swung around to close the door, nearly tripping over the pup, who was glued to his heels. "Watch out now," he said. Then,

"D'you know where I put Michelle's card?"

Suleka pointed across at his desk from where she was lighting the burner under the kettle on the stove.

"Ah." Lange strode across the room, snatched up the card, and swung around to go back outside, where his cell phone could pick up a signal. He nearly tripped over the terrier a second time. "I think I've made a friend here," he said to Suleka.

"As long as he's not too young for you," she quipped.

He glared at her as he closed the door. Max immediately started to whine. Lange tapped Michelle's number into his phone and trotted down the steps as he hit the "call" button. He bounced toward his log pile, feeling a definite flutter of excitement that he'd be hearing her voice.

"Pate-Swenson," she answered.

"Hi. This is Callum Lange."

"Callum, great. Perfect timing. Forensics are still working the scene up here, but they just loaded Doyle into the coroner's Suburban."

Lange became all business. "Did she assess a cause of death?"

"Tomeoka? Not exactly. She said there's a significant blow to the back of his head, a contusion on his forehead, but she also suspects some neck trauma, so she wants to hold off on a final cause until the pathologist does the autopsy. How did it go for you with the wife?"

"It wasn't my finest hour," confessed Lange. "But look, I'm on my way back up, so I'll tell you about it when I get there. And I have Suleka with me. Is now a good time for her to come talk to you?"

"Perfect."

"Great. We have information to share."

"Me, too."

"Okay. See you in a bit." Lange swung around to head back to the yurt, then thought of something. "Oh and hey," he said into the phone, but there was no reply. He looked at his screen and saw the call had ended. No matter, he thought, he'd take the dog with him and leave him in the truck if they didn't want him out.

He heard the kettle whistling on the stove before he even opened the door to the yurt. Suleka was on her knees in the kitchen, dabbing at Max's wound with wet cotton, a bag of sliced ham open on the counter above them. "That looks much better," he said as he turned off the gas under the kettle and filled the filter on his ceramic coffeepot with boiling water. Suleka had already put the ground French roast in the cloth filter, and the sharp tang of good coffee filled the air around him.

"I had to bribe him to get him away from the door," said Suleka, finishing up. She stopped dabbing at the dog and clutched the edge of the counter with one hand to pull herself back up.

The dog limped over to Lange and sat. Lange leaned down and stroked his head.

"Whatever got him must have bruised his shoulder, because he's pretty tender there," said Suleka. "Darn," she added, looking down at the saucer of warm water and accumulation of bloody cotton balls she'd left on the floor. "I should have grabbed those before I stood up."

"Is your back bothering you again?"

"Little bit today," Suleka admitted.

"I'll clean that up," said Lange. He refilled the filter on the coffeepot, then set about gathering up the remnants of wound care.

"Did you get through to your DEA friend?" Suleka asked, washing her hands at the kitchen sink.

Lange didn't bother correcting her this time. He knew she'd tease him until he and Michelle Pate-Swenson actually became friends. If they became friends. Then she'd back off. "Yep. She's expecting us."

"Okay, I'll put the coffee in to-go cups."

They switched places so Lange could trash the cotton balls and rinse his own hands. "Should we take milk? What if she doesn't drink it black?"

Suleka nodded across at a small cooler. "I put a jelly jar of milk in that with all the baked goods. And a couple of packets of sugar."

"Good thinking!" Lange dried his hands on a dish towel, peering down into the cooler. He suddenly felt shy. "You don't think I'll look . . . you know . . . forward, taking her lunch?"

Suleka tipped her head as she looked at him, compassion replacing her usual sassiness. "I think you'll look very thoughtful," she assured him.

He gave a curt nod of his head to cover his embarrassment, then looked down at the dog. "We have to feed him."

"He drank the first saucer of water I put down to clean his wound, and then he ate some of the ham. I don't know what else you've got that we can give him."

Lange stepped to the fridge, Max on his heels. "I have some leftover cooked burger meat and rice . . ."

"Er, no, you don't. Those were both pretty furry, so I chucked them."

"What should we do then?"

Suleka looked at Max. "He doesn't look unhappy to me."

"So we wait?"

"Till you have something more appropriate to feed him, I would."

"Okay, then let's go. You, too," he said down to Max.

Once they got on the road, though, Lange told Suleka that he planned to leave the terrier in the Nissan while he checked with Collins whether it was okay to let him out. "I was going to ask Michelle," he told her, as she pulled in tight behind one of the many green sheriff's vehicles parked in front of the yellow gate. "But we hung up too fast."

He climbed out, a coffee in each hand, and bumped the door closed with his hip. He heard Max whine as he started toward the abandoned logging road. Michelle was walking toward him, Kojak trotting beside her.

"Hi there," she called and Lange slowed, enjoying her smile. "I thought I'd come to you because Collins and the deputies are having a confab that doesn't involve me. Is that coffee?" she asked, leaning forward and waving the aroma toward her.

"Yes, and we brought you a cup," replied Lange, thrusting one of the cups at the agent.

"Oh thank you, thank you!" exclaimed Michelle, eagerly taking the insulated cup from his hand.

Lange nodded back toward the Nissan. "We have milk, too, if you need it."

"Wow! You thought of everything."

"Oh no, not me," Lange confessed, swiveling around to point out Suleka, who was coming around the front of the Nissan, carrying the cooler. "That lady there is who thought of most everything. My friend and co-investigator."

"Suleka, right?" said Michelle, stepping forward, one hand outstretched to shake. "Thanks for being willing to talk to me."

"You're welcome," said Suleka. She set the cooler down and wiped her right hand on her jean overalls before shaking. "We brought some lunch, too, in case you're hungry. Cal thought you might not eat gluten, so we got everything at the gluten-free bakery."

Michelle half closed one eye and tipped her head, looking at Lange. "How did you . . . ?"

He tapped the side of his nose with his forefinger. "I used to be a detective."

Michelle laughed, and the intensity of the day seemed to dissipate with the sound. "I'm impressed." She looked down at the cooler, then back up at Suleka. "And yes, I am gluten-free, I do take milk in my coffee, and I'm *famished*."

"Great," said Suleka. "Maybe we can find a place to sit and eat and talk at the same time."

"Sure. There's a couple of stumps over by the gate . . . ," said Michelle. She glanced across at the Nissan. "What're you doing?" she called out. Kojak was sitting by the vehicle, staring up at the passenger-side window.

"He's eyeing Bob Doyle's terrier, Max," explained Lange.

"Who must have run off after Bob died, 'cause I found him hiding under my yurt. Is it okay to let him out?"

"Sure," said Michelle.

"I don't suppose you have any dog food, do you?" Suleka asked.

"As a matter of fact, I do. I always bring some in case the day stretches out too long for Kojak."

Lange could see the group around Collins breaking up. He walked away from the women as they started toward Michelle's Range Rover, feeling pretty sure that they were comfortable without him now.

"That's your dog's name? Kojak?" he heard Suleka ask from behind him. "Are you even old enough to have watched *Kojak* when it was on TV?"

Lange spun his head around, to give Suleka a warning look about prying into Michelle's age, but both women were engrossed in each other.

"I'm fifty-one, so yes," answered Michelle. "I watched every episode."

And Lange suddenly felt that flutter of excitement again.

CHAPTER 7

He hoofed it around the yellow gate and passed two guys walking toward him. They were wearing simple shirts and jeans but had paper booties over their shoes, so he guessed they were from forensics. He nodded a greeting and stole a glance at their evidence bags, but they were deep in conversation, so they didn't pay attention to him.

"What d'you find?" he asked Collins, who was standing alone by the downed fir tree, having released his two deputies. It was the first time Lange had seen Collins in a suit and tie. "Congratulations, by the way."

"On what?" asked Collins. There were small beads of sweat on his forehead, and Lange imagined he was hot in his suit, which he was required to wear to set him apart from the uniformed deputies.

"On making detective."

"Oh. Yes. Thanks." The thick-bodied thirtysomething detective cracked a smile, and Lange realized it was the first time he'd seen him do that, too. "How did it go with Mrs. Doyle?" Collins asked.

Lange filled him in on the conversation at the Doyle house and René's advancing dementia.

"Had she even figured out that Bob didn't come home last night?" Collins asked.

"Not that I could tell. She seemed fixated on the idea that he was outside with Kevin, cutting up a fir log, even though Kevin was in the room with us."

"Were you able to get her to understand that Bob was dead?"

"I wasn't." Lange looked down at his feet, the sound of René's howl coming back to him. "Kevin was, though."

Collins clucked ruefully, a faraway look in his eyes. "I told my wife, if I ever get to a place like that, take me hiking up in the mountains and let me get lost."

Lange blinked at such a revelation from this young, solidly built detective who breathed like his nose was plugged all the time. "I didn't know you were a hiker," he remarked.

"Used to be," said Collins. "Used to be my favorite thing to do with my wife." His eyes took on that faraway look again. "We went on more'n one hike where we ended up getting turned around together, and I still get a kick out of that." His focus came back to Lange, his tone matter-of-fact. "I've got Alzheimer's on both sides of my family, and I'd rather be in a place where I think I'm out with my wife than in a place where I can't think who my wife is."

He paused, the air heavy with breezeless heat around them, then looked down at the spiral notebook in his hand. "Okay, so our drug-sniffing K9 marked three places on this road." He pointed with his pen toward the ditch beside them. "The first was here, where Kojak found the white powder. Forensics took a sample of that." His pen moved to indicate farther up the road. "The second was on the road just out a ways from Doyle's body."

"Was there a rock on the road in that place?"

"Yes. Agent Pate-Swenson said she thought you might have put it there."

"I did. Because Kojak came back to it twice."

"We couldn't *see* anything there . . ."

"Me, either."

"But I had forensics take a sample from the surface of the road because I trust the K9s."

Lange nodded his agreement.

"Here's what we know," Collins went on, stepping closer to the small fir tree lying at an angle from the uphill bank down across the road. "Something went down both here and up by Doyle's body. Here, in addition to the check with the bloody fingerprint on it, we found some blood on this broken branch." He pointed with his pen at the jagged end coming out of the tree's trunk.

Lange leaned over and saw the brownish stains. "Clarkson turned up at work yesterday with a swollen lip and a cut on his forehead," he told Collins.

Collins took this in. "Could be someone punched him and he fell sideways onto this?" he suggested, still pointing at the blood on the broken branch. "But whether that happened before or after Bob Doyle got killed is anybody's guess."

"You're sure Doyle was murdered then?" asked Lange.

"Looks that way. Somebody hit him in the face and he fell backward onto the rock. Either blow could have killed him."

"Did you get a time of death?"

"Tomeoka guessed early in the morning yesterday. But she said to wait for the autopsy."

"Okay, so how about this?" began Lange, climbing over the downed fir and marching Collins up the road toward the blackberries. "Bob Doyle is up here with Kevin and Kyle, trying to talk his grandson out of getting involved in this drug stuff. Clarkson just wants to get the drugs and get out of here, so he punches the older Doyle, snatches up the shipment, and starts down the road. Kevin wants to help his grandpa but he's also flaming mad at Clarkson, so he chases after Kyle and they fight down by the tree."

"You're thinking Wayne Clarkson wasn't part of this?"

They'd arrived at the blackberries, and Lange was looking back down the road, toward the fir tree. His eyes glazed over as he thought. He was trying to get a feel as to what had happened here, but the air was still around him, and faintly winey from the warm, ripe blackberries.

"Lange?"

"I can see both Clarksons here more easily than I can see Kevin Doyle," he admitted finally.

"Because?"

"Because Kevin looked genuinely devastated when I told him his grandfather was dead. And the way he takes care of his grandmother, I don't see him leaving Bob to die in this ditch." Lange stroked his jaw with his hand. "You said your dog marked a third place."

"Yes." The young detective started walking Lange back toward the fir tree. "Again, we couldn't see anything there, either, although we did find something interesting close by. We're just not sure it's relevant."

"What was it?"

"A nine-millimeter cartridge lodged in the road. We might never have seen it, but one of the deputies needed to take a leak and dropped over the bank to find someplace private. When he came back up, the road was at eye level and the ambient light must have hit it just right for him to notice this groove on the surface." He stopped and pointed down at a short pencil line in the gravel surface of the road, with a hole at the end of it.

Lange heard a plaintive whine and looked up to see Max standing on top of the downed fir, leaning forward like he wanted to spring into Lange's arms. "That's Bob Doyle's dog," he told Collins.

"Bob Doyle had a dog?"

"Uh-huh. And he was up here with him yesterday."

"How d'you know?"

"He ended up at my place, hiding." A thought suddenly occurred to Lange. "Don't dogs usually stay with their masters if there's a problem?"

"Depends," shrugged Collins. "He's only a little guy, so maybe hunger got the better of him."

"I s'pose. He had a fresh wound on his right shoulder, so maybe he came looking for help after he tore himself up."

Collins made a small hmmm of doubt. "Dogs are pretty stoic when it comes to that kind of thing. It's more likely he was chased off by whoever was here yesterday."

"Which, again, makes me think Kevin wasn't here," said Lange.

"Why?"

"Because he would've just taken Max home with him."

The dog whined again.

"Mind if I call him over?" asked Lange.

"No. Go right ahead."

Lange threw his left arm out and motioned it back toward himself. "Come on, Max. Come."

The dog didn't move.

Kojak leapt over the little fir tree, leading Michelle and Suleka. "You want this one?" asked Michelle, scooping Max up in her arms as she climbed over the tree.

"Thanks." Lange smiled.

She started walking toward him, but Max twisted and scrabbled in her arms so frantically she finally let him down. He ran right back to his position on the fir tree.

"Why doesn't he want to come over?" wondered Lange out loud.

"That is strange," said Suleka, coming up alongside Lange.

"He and Kojak were playing so well together," Michelle added, looking down at her German shepherd.

"You don't think . . . ?" said Collins to Lange. He looked down at the ground, where the bullet had been, then back up at Max.

"Oh, now that's a thought," Lange concurred.

"What?" asked Michelle.

Collins took two steps across the road, toward the ditch on the uphill side. "Our K9 marked this spot," he said, pointing close to his feet, where a patch of small alders had encroached on the road. "What if whoever killed Doyle was taking off with the drugs and the dog came after him, making him drop the shipment . . ."

". . . so he shot at the dog and clipped him," finished Lange, looking back at Max.

"I can't see Kevin shooting Max any more than I can see him killing his grandfather," Suleka warned them all.

"At this point I agree with you," confessed Lange. "We're thinking it was Kyle."

"The thing is," interjected Collins, "we ran a check on Kyle Clarkson and there's no violence on his record. His brother, on the other hand . . ."

"See, that's what I'm thinking," said Suleka, wagging her finger at Collins like he was right. "Substitute Wayne Clarkson for Kyle in your little scenario, and I'd say you're on to something."

"But we found that check made out to Kyle," said Michelle.

"So maybe it was just the two brothers," suggested Collins, "and Kyle does what you said Kevin did. He comes up to get the drugs with his brother but gets into a fight with him after Wayne kills Bob Doyle. Or maybe even after Wayne shoots at the dog, because guns weren't supposed to be part of their deal?"

"But then I come back to why is Doyle here if Kevin isn't somehow involved?" argued Lange.

"Unless he was just out for a walk with his dog," said Suleka.

They all turned and looked at her in syncopated silence, contemplating this possibility as it grew on them in value.

"But if *that's* the case," theorized Lange, looking back toward the yellow gate, "then where's Bob Doyle's pickup truck?"

CHAPTER 8

"Time to question the Clarksons," announced Collins, flipping the top of his notebook closed and slipping it in his jacket pocket.

"Can I come with you?" asked Michelle.

The detective nodded. "Sure. Aren't we all going?"

"I'd like to go talk to Kyle Clarkson's ex-wife, if you don't mind," said Lange.

"Why?"

Lange told Collins of his conversation with Jen at Albert's, Suleka adding her details to fill out what they knew.

"Then yeah," agreed Collins. "I think talking to Brandie sounds like a great idea. Do you know where she lives?"

"I do," said Suleka, her hand up in the air. "She's right in Rockport."

"The Clarksons, too," said Collins. "Wayne's on Highway 530, just outside of Rockport, but close enough." He looked at his watch. "It's almost two now. Let's meet at Steelhead Park, by the old pioneer cabin there, once we're all done. You know where I mean, right?"

"I do," said Lange. "But what if you've got cause to arrest one of the Clarksons?"

"Then I'll call you."

"Okay."

They all started toward the fir tree.

"Do you know what kind of pickup Robert Doyle drove?" Collins asked as he stepped over the small tree.

"A Ford half ton," said Lange.

"White," added Suleka. "Although you might not know it's white under all the dirt."

Lange picked up Max on his way over the fir, then put him back on the ground. "Wasn't the tailgate a different color?" he asked.

"That's right. With a blue tailgate," Suleka amended.

"That should make it easy to spot," said Collins. "I'll put out an instant message for law enforcement to keep an eye out for it."

They were strolling toward the yellow gate, two abreast, as if out for an afternoon walk on pleasant summer day. Inside their heads, Lange imagined, they were all turning the case over, running a list of questions they might ask the suspects alongside a list of things to watch for in the responses. In the short term, however, they were taking a moment to soak up the faint, citrusy odor coming from the foliage around them and enjoy the peace of a stroll on the mountain.

"What do you want to do about Max?" asked Suleka when she and Lange were together in the Nissan, headed down Sauk Mountain Road. Collins and Michelle were ahead of them in their respective vehicles, and Suleka had to hang back not to breathe too much road dust. She and Lange both had their windows open.

Max sat between them, oblivious to the road dust.

"What do you mean?" Lange asked.

"Should we drop him off at your place?"

"There's no point. We'd just have to come back up to fetch him to take him over to René's."

"You think she'll want him?"

"Who, René? I'm sure she will. Don't you think?"

"I don't know." Suleka glanced at the little pup. Somehow she couldn't imagine him wanting to leave Lange. She reached her right hand out and scratched the dog on the top of his head as she closed the distance between Sauk Mountain Road and Rockport.

Just three short minutes later, she pulled into the short, steep driveway at the little house in Rockport where Brandie Clarkson lived. Lange bounded out of the Nissan and crossed to the front door in one fluid move. Suleka followed.

The door was open and Lange could see a young woman, maybe in her late twenties, sitting at the kitchen table, playing with her phone.

"Hello, Brandie?" he inquired from outside.

The woman spun her head in his direction, surprised by the interruption. "Hello?" she asked back. She put her phone on the table and jumped up, crossing the living room to come to the front door. Lange noticed that she was petite and dark haired, like her mother, with the same full lips. Her face had an elfin quality, even with the deep furrow of distrust he'd caused in her brow.

"I'm Callum Lange and this is my associate, Suleka . . ." Lange started.

The young woman's brow cleared. "Oh, you're the detective who wants to talk to me," she acknowledged. "My mom texted and said you might be over. She also said not to tell anyone so don't worry, I didn't. If my ex has been up to his old BS, I want to know about it. I'm certainly not gonna give him a heads-up. Come on in," she said, waving them into her tidy and, in its own way, charming little house.

"We're not sure what he's been up to yet, if anything, but we are curious about what happened yesterday that left him with a fat lip."

"That's why he wouldn't look at me?" questioned Brandie, her brown eyes bright with anger. "I knew it wasn't good when Alice said that Uncle Wayne had stopped them from driving up to the fish hatchery like they planned." She tossed her head up with enough force that her short, dark ponytail flickered side to side. "Did you go talk to Kyle and Wayne yet?"

"A Skagit County sheriff's detective is on his way over to both their houses right now. With a DEA agent."

"DEA?" quizzed Brandie. "This is about drugs?"

"Partly, yes," said Lange, knowing it was best to give her everything so she could help them approach Alice with their questions.

Brandie's eyes got steely. "What's the other part?"

Suleka reached forward and touched the young woman on the arm. "We found a dead body up there."

Brandie's eyes shifted back to Lange, fear replacing bravado.

"Dead like someone OD'd? Oh no!" she said, imagining the worst. "It wasn't Wayne, was it? I hope my Alice didn't have to see something like that."

"No, it was Robert Doyle," Suleka told her.

"Robert *Doyle*?" Brandie repeated. "What's he got to do with drugs? Or is this something to do with Kevin somehow?"

"We don't know," said Lange. "We don't even know who was up on Sauk at the time this all happened."

"What time was that?"

"Sometime after six a.m."

"That doesn't narrow it down much," scoffed Brandie.

Lange couldn't help but smile. He liked this young woman's quick mind and forthrightness.

"If it helps," she went on, "I dropped Alice off at Kyle's at eight thirty, on my way to work. And I know they were planning to head up to the hatchery around nine. So if Wayne was gonna lead Kyle on some felony when *Alice* was with him, then he would've had to turn up between eight thirty and nine."

Lange turned this over in his mind. The coroner had suggested the time of death was "early in the morning." If early meant before eight thirty, that could let Kyle out. "That does help, yes."

There was quiet for a moment in the cheerfully decorated living room, as they all thought their various thoughts. Then a vehicle with a muffler problem growled past on the street outside and brought them back to each other. "Can we talk to Alice?" Lange asked.

"Yes. Yes, you can. As long as I can stay with her."

"Of course."

Brandie crossed to a door off the living room, opened it, and called up. "Alice!" She looked back at Lange and Suleka. "You might not get much out of her, though, even with me there. She's been real quiet since yesterday. Alice!" she called out again.

"Is she in her room?" Lange asked.

Brandie nodded.

"Then maybe we should go to her. She might feel more

comfortable talking there."

"Okay, sure." Brandie led them both up a narrow flight of walled-in stairs to a small bedroom with a sloping ceiling and two dormer windows with views out to the Skagit River.

Alice Clarkson was sitting on a single bed under the windows, leaning up against an array of Disney character pillows and stuffed toys. She was coloring in a book balanced on her knees, listening to music through earbuds. As soon as her mother walked into the room, she pulled out one of the earbuds from under her long, shiny brown hair. "What?" she said.

"Honey, these people have come to talk to you about yesterday," said her mother, perching on the bed next to Alice. Suleka walked to the end of the bed, and Lange stayed by the door so he wouldn't have to bend to stand under the ceiling.

Alice looked from one to the other of the strangers, her hazel-green eyes wide with curiosity.

"My name's Cal and this is Suleka," said Lange, trying to put the little girl at ease. She didn't look discontented sitting amongst her things in her room, just a little anxious. "We were hoping you could tell us where you went with your dad yesterday?"

Alice shrugged. "Nowhere," she said, then looked at her mom.

"Did you go up Sauk with Uncle Wayne?" asked Brandie.

Lange wished she hadn't been quite so direct but yielded to her authority as the parent.

"No-o," argued Alice, then tried to cover her hostility by coloring again.

Brandie slipped a loving arm around her daughter. "It's okay, sweetie. You can tell us."

But Alice shrugged her off. "There's nothing to tell, Mom." She made direct eye contact with her mother. "Honest!"

Lange saw her eyes widen with the word and wondered if she was trying to send her mother a message not to ask in front of him.

"But your Uncle Wayne did come over to your dad's yesterday while you were there?" he asked the eight-year-old.

Alice gave him a half-hearted shrug and a nod, but she didn't make eye contact.

"And did you go out for a ride somewhere together?"

Alice stared down at the page in her coloring book. When she lifted her eyes away from it again, it was to look out the window, then around to her mother. "Can I go get an apple and some peanut butter?"

Brandie hesitated, assessing the situation. She pulled her daughter in closer and kissed the side of her head. "Sure," she said.

Alice dropped her coloring book, pulled off the other earbud, and fled.

Brandie looked at Lange. "I'm sorry," she said. "That's about as much as I've been able to get out of her since her dad dropped her off yesterday, and I can't tell if she's trying to protect him or if that lowlife brother of his scared her somehow."

"You think Wayne might have driven her up Sauk?"

She sniffed and folded her arms across her chest belligerently. "Last I knew Wayne's rig was broke down."

"So it would have been Kyle's vehicle they were in," acknowledged Lange. "What does Kyle drive?"

"A red Toyota pickup."

Lange looked across at Suleka.

"What?" asked Brandie.

He lifted his shoulders, not wanting to say.

"Oh, don't give me that!" complained Brandie. "It's bad enough I gotta take it from an eight-year-old. You should at least be straight with me."

"You're right," agreed Lange. "I had a red Toyota pickup fly past me coming down Sauk Mountain yesterday."

"And there were two men in it?"

Lange paused, remembering back to the way the vehicle had almost spun him around, it had gone by at such speed. He'd stood shaking his fist at it; did he see the backs of two heads behind the seats? "No," he answered. "There was only one."

Brandie's cheeks flexed as she gritted her teeth at this news. "Well, maybe it was Wayne took off with Kyle's pickup, and that's what's got Alice scared." Now she shrugged, too. "Or it could've been somebody different. There's a lot of red Toyota pickups out there."

"That's true," conceded Lange.

Brandie sighed and her eyes filled with sadness. "Truth is, I don't want it to be Kyle. We're not married anymore but we're friends. And he's a real good dad to Alice."

Lange decided not to tell her about the check. He dug in the back pocket of his jeans and pulled out a business card. "Can you call me if you get Alice to open up?"

Brandie took the card. "Sure. What is it you want to know exactly?"

"If she was up on Sauk yesterday with her dad. Once we know that, we might be able to get the rest of the story to fall into place."

They parted company down in the living room again, where Alice was at the kitchen table playing with her mother's phone while she bit into a slice of apple. Lange and Suleka walked slowly over the front lawn to the Nissan. "What is it with me today?" he asked. "I feel like I've completely lost my ability to get people to talk to me."

"She's just scared, is all," said Suleka. Max was on the passenger side of the Nissan, standing on his hind legs, his front paws up on the door, and Suleka could see that he'd been worrying the wound on his shoulder. It gave her an idea. "Go back in with Max," she told Lange.

He gave her a look, like he didn't get it. "Why?"

"I don't know," she answered. "I just have a feeling."

Lange paused, contemplating her suggestion. He glanced across at the front door. "What pretext will I use?"

Suleka reached into the pickup, lifted Max out, and thrust him at Lange. "You'll come up with something," she said.

Lange strode the few steps back over to the house, Suleka

behind him. He set Max down on the porch. “Hello?” he called out.

“Did you forget something?” Brandie said, rounding the corner toward the door just as Max skittered up over the threshold and into the living room.

“Kind of,” Lange said, stepping in after the dog.

But Alice overrode him. She gasped, leapt down from the table, and almost slid across the wood floor on her knees to throw her arms around Max. “You’re okay!” she squealed.

And just like that Lange knew where Alice had been the day before.

CHAPTER 9

Suleka backed the Nissan out of the driveway and headed down the hill toward Steelhead Park. The Skagit River lay below them, its calm green surface like sleepy cat's eyes, enticing her to step in and cool off awhile, but she knew it was actually moving at a pace that could scare anyone standing in it. A few RVs were dotted about here and there throughout the park, and a heavy-duty blue Ford pickup with a matching canopy was backing a powerboat down the ramp, to go out on the river. She stopped at the bottom of the hill by the post office and looked right to see two women and a golden retriever on a leash, heading down the trail alongside the river. She looked left and could see Michelle's silver Range Rover and the green bumper of Collins's Ford Interceptor sedan poking out on the other side of it. They were both standing on the grass by the centuries-old wood pioneer cabin, talking.

"Did you find the Clarksons?" Suleka called out to Michelle through her open window as she pulled in to park beside the Range Rover.

Lange rolled out as soon as the Nissan stopped moving, Max at his heels, and Kojak, who had been fully involved in sniffing the grass around the cabin, leapt excitedly to play with Max.

"We found Kyle," said Michelle.

"But nobody was home at Wayne's," Collins added. "His Jeep was there, though."

"That's probably because it's not functioning," Lange said.

"You know that for sure?" asked Collins.

"That's what Brandie told me. And it makes sense of why he went over to Kyle's in the first place. If he needed to pick up the drug shipment, he'd need a vehicle to get up Sauk."

"And Kyle might not have trusted him just to take his," said Suleka. "So he went up with him and took Alice."

The dogs tumbled over and around each other, chasing and nipping and teasing and tugging.

"Brandie said she didn't drop Alice off till eight thirty," said Lange, "which may be after the early-morning guesstimate that the coroner gave for time of death."

"So maybe Wayne killed him and then went and got Kyle?" suggested Michelle.

"To help him move the body," Collins proposed. "Except, then how did Wayne get up Sauk in the first place?"

"Kevin?" said Michelle.

An SUV with a canoe on top of it drove into the park behind them, but none of them paid attention to it. They were all trying to arrange the pieces of the puzzle to make them fit.

"So Wayne gets a ride from Kevin," Collins hypothesized once the SUV turned down toward the boat landing. "To pick up the drugs."

"And Bob Doyle gets wind of it and goes after them," continues Michelle. "There's a fight, Bob ends up dead, and Kevin says he's not going to move the body. Wayne's on his own for that. So Wayne goes after Kyle."

"But would Kevin go to the trouble of dropping Wayne at his brother's place?" asked Suleka, unconvinced.

"How about this," said Lange. "Wayne gets a ride from Kevin up Sauk, but Kevin hightails it out of there as soon as he figures out it's to pick up drugs. He wants no part of that. He misses his grandfather, who's found out somehow that the two of them were headed up Sauk, and Bob Doyle ends up confronting Wayne alone. Wayne punches him, Bob falls, and Wayne takes off with the drugs."

"How did he get down the mountain?" asked Michelle.

"He stole Bob's truck. That's why he went to get Kyle. He needed him to go back up the mountain with him so he could dump the truck back there now that he didn't need it anymore."

Collins exhaled noisily and they all looked at him. "You're assuming he didn't think Bob Doyle was dead."

"Correct."

"So then why isn't Bob Doyle's truck still parked at the gate on Sauk?"

"Maybe they went in to check on Bob, and as soon as they figured out he was dead, Kyle took off because *he* didn't want any part of *that*!" Suleka conjectured.

"Ohhhh, Wayne wouldn't want them checking on Bob Doyle," countered Michelle. "Not only did Bob confront Wayne about the drugs, if Lange's version is correct, but then Wayne punched Bob *and* stole his pick up truck. No way he would want them going anywhere *near* Bob Doyle." She looked at Lange. "Don't you think?"

Max yelped, and they all turned to see the roughhousing between the dogs at a sudden end. Max picked himself up and limped back toward Lange as Kojak rolled onto his back and scratched in the grass.

Lange leaned down and picked up the pup. "I do," he said in answer to Michelle's question. Max was licking him on the chin, and Lange gently cupped his muzzle and moved it, stroking the dog's nose with his thumb. He looked down at the Jack Russell and said, "Plus we still have to figure out how this one came into it."

"Did you find anything out from Alice Clarkson?" asked Collins, bringing them all back to the point of this meeting.

"Well, she was definitely up on Sauk yesterday," answered Suleka. "Because she was surprised to see Max still alive."

"So she knows who shot at him?" asked Michelle.

"Yep," replied Lange. "But she wasn't saying."

"Neither was Kyle."

"No?"

Collins joined in. "He told us he didn't know anything about being up on Sauk yesterday, and when I asked him what happened to his face, he said he got hit with some lumber at the mill yesterday."

"But he turned up at work looking like that," argued Suleka.

"That's what Lange said," Collins acknowledged. "But I wasn't about to admit I knew that. Not yet, anyways. I wanted Kyle to tell the truth without me forcing it." Collins's eyes shifted away. He let out a long, almost sad-sounding breath before shifting them back. "Kyle's turned his life around in the last few years. I guess I wanted to give him the chance to prove he hasn't fallen back."

"His ex said something similar," said Lange.

"You might be better off telling him that," Suleka remarked to Collins. "'Cause I'm not sure he's bright enough to get there by himself."

Lange looked at his straight-talking associate. "Maybe it's time we went and saw Kyle Clarkson. If we tell him that whatever happened is weighing on Alice, he might live up to these guys' belief in him tell us the truth so she won't have to."

"Can I come along?" asked Michelle. "If you don't mind," she added quickly, her right hand out, fingers up, toward Suleka. "I'm just thinking if you do go back to Alice, I'd like Kojak to be there." She looked across at her dog, who was following a butterfly with his nose in the air. "Dogs can really relax a child when they're talking to law enforcement."

They all looked at Collins. "'S'fine with me," he said. "Kyle told me he thought Wayne might be holed up at his girlfriend's place on the Rockport-Cascade Road, so I was gonna go over there next. Why don't you call me after you've talked with Kyle, and we'll see where we're at?"

CHAPTER 10

They took both vehicles the short distance to Clarkson's double-wide, and Michelle parked her Range Rover on the street because there wasn't enough room in the driveway next to the Nissan. Lange watched her hop down and tease some of her blonde hair back toward the braid at the back of her head. He looked away so as not to intrude and found Suleka watching him.

"You should ask her out," she muttered.

Lange gave her a stern look: *enough!*

"Okay, I'll shut up," she said. Then she treated him to a smirk.

Lange puckered indignantly but found himself smiling in his own way, too.

"We ready?" asked Michelle, coming up to join them.

Lange nodded. He led the way to the front door, which, like at Brandie's house, was wide open, the television blaring a baseball game in the background.

"Hello!" he called out.

The game stopped abruptly, and he heard a mechanical *thwang*, like the footrest on a recliner being pushed down. A tall, big-bodied man appeared in front of them. Clarkson was not fat so much as fleshy and out of shape, with unruly brown hair that was presently covering the cut on his temple. But not the black eye that was beginning to emerge as a result of that cut. He had overnight stubble on his cheeks and chin, a diet soda in his right hand, and the left side of his mouth looked like it was holding a big wad of chewing tobacco, it was so swollen. "What?" he said, his eyes bouncing from Suleka to Lange. Then they bounced back to Michelle, and he shifted his weight. "Did you find my brother already?" he asked, a worry line creasing his forehead.

"Detective Collins is on his way to see if he can find him now," said Lange. "But we were hoping you might answer a few questions for us. My name's Callum Lange and this is—"

"I know who you are," interrupted Kyle. "And I already told Mike that I don't know nothing about anything that happened up on Sauk yesterday."

This was the first time Lange had heard Collins called by his first name, and he guessed that the two men had been in the same class at school. He knew Collins was raised in the Upper Skagit, and it was possible he was the same age as Kyle. "The thing is, Mr. Clarkson," he said, staying on the doorstep. "Your daughter, Alice, *does* know something about the happenings on Sauk yesterday and—"

"You talked to her?!" interrupted Kyle angrily. "I didn't say you could talk to her. Don't you need my permission or something?"

"We had her mother's permission."

Kyle shook his head from side to side, like this bothered him. "She should'a asked me first."

"She's worried about Alice," Suleka put in, "and you should be, too, Kyle." She stepped up into the trailer to stand next to him. Lange and Michelle held their places outside. Suleka touched Clarkson on the forearm to get his full attention. "Whatever went down up there has got Alice scared, and she's not her usual happy self. Is that what you want for her?"

Kyle shook his head no again but didn't say anything. He'd been meeting Suleka's eye but now he looked away, ashamed. She stepped in closer.

"If you don't tell us what happened," she said, "we're going to have to pry it out of Alice. You don't want that, do you?"

There was a long beat of silence, broken only by the sound of children shrieking happily as they played on the jungle gym at the park below.

"You think it would help if we told it together?" Kyle asked, bringing his eyes back to Suleka. "So she could say what scared her. Would that, like, help her get it out? And move on?"

"I think that would help a lot," agreed Suleka.

"Alright," agreed Clarkson and Lange saw his shoulders relax with relief. "Let me get my shoes on."

Five minutes later they were all standing on Brandie's doorstep, Lange holding Max in his arms and Kojak on a leash next to Michelle.

"Oh. You're back," said Brandie, coming around the corner from the kitchen into the living room as soon as she heard their commotion. Her eyes fixed on Kyle, steely, hard, then she turned her head back toward the kitchen. "Alice," she said, "your dad's here."

The eight-year-old flew around the corner, hair flapping behind her. "Daddy!" she cried and landed with a bump into his belly, clasping her arms around his waist. He leaned down and pulled her into a fierce hug with his big arms.

"It's okay, honey," he said, kissing her on the top of her head. "It's gonna be okay."

Alice looked up at him. "But . . . ?"

"We're just gonna answer some questions for these guys, 'kay? We'll do it together."

Alice shifted her eyes from him to her mother. Brandie nodded. "Okay," Alice told her dad. He walked her over to the couch and sat her down next to him.

"Well, you'd better come on in," said Brandie to the rest of them.

"Is it okay if we bring the dogs in?" asked Michelle.

"Sure. I don't mind."

Lange set Max down and he scampered over to Alice, who immediately reached forward and stroked his ears, avoiding eye contact with everyone else. Lange and Suleka entered and stood to the left of the front door, at an angle facing the couch, in front of the TV, leaving Michelle the small armchair to one side of Alice. Michelle didn't hesitate. She went and made herself at home, putting Kojak between her and Alice. "Sit," she told the German shepherd.

Kojak sat.

Brandie carried a kitchen chair over for Suleka.

"I'm fine," said Lange, one hand up in the air.

"You're sure?" she asked.

"Uh-huh." He put a foot up on the back rung of Suleka's chair to show he was comfortable.

Alice sneaked a peek at Michelle's dog.

"His name is Kojak," said the DEA agent.

"Can I pet him?" asked Alice, peeking at Michelle now.

"Sure. Thanks for asking."

"My dad said I should always ask," said Alice, her small hand gently dusting the fur on the back of Kojak's head. "'Cause not every dog is friendly."

"That's true," said Michelle. "Good advice."

Kojak tipped his head up, enjoying her touch. Max stood on his hind legs, both front paws on Alice's knee, so she could pet him, too. Kojak swung his muzzle around and placed it on her other knee, not to be left out. Alice giggled.

Everyone smiled at the sound, releasing some of the tension in the room. Kyle looked at Lange. Lange nodded.

He turned back to look at his daughter. "Alice, honey, we have to tell these people what happened with Uncle Wayne yesterday."

Alice looked up at her dad, her face serious but trusting. "Even though Uncle Wayne said not to?"

Brandie bristled beside Michelle, and Michelle slipped her hand in the young mother's. Brandie perched on the arm of Michelle's chair.

"Yeah, even though Uncle Wayne said not to," said Kyle. "Because we don't keep secrets like that, right?"

"Right," agreed his daughter. "Can I put Max on my lap?"

"I guess," said her father.

"I think he'd like that," said Lange and for the first time, Alice smiled across at him. She tapped her lap and Max leapt up, making her giggle again.

Kyle kept his eyes down on her petting Max as he started his narrative, obviously uncomfortable being in the spotlight. "So Alice and me were gonna go up to the fish hatchery yesterday," he said. "After we had our morning snack together. Then Wayne showed up. He said—he *said*," Kyle emphasized, looking at Lange now, like he wanted him to be sure this was how he heard the story, "that him and his girlfriend had gone up Sauk to see the sunrise and she accidentally hit a deer on the way down."

"Like your brother would drag himself outta bed for a sunrise!" scoffed Brandie.

"I know. I *know*," agreed Kyle testily. "I figured they'd maybe got, you know . . ." He glanced at Alice, but she was busy playing with Max and Kojak, so he made a sign above her head, finger and thumb to his lips, to suggest they were stoned. "And that's how come they hit a deer. Either that or he poached one. Anyway, he said he needed my truck to go get this deer. I said, 'How come you didn't bring it out in Tosha's?'—his girlfriend's—and he said, ''Cause she couldn't wait. She had to get to work.' And I know his Jeep needs a new head gasket, so I said, 'Okay, but you're not taking my truck. I'll drive you up there.'

"'Nah,' he said, 'just gimme the truck.'

"But I said, 'No way! You'll be gone with it all day. And I won't even drive you if Alice says she don't wanna go, because I'm not leaving her here by herself.'"

"I said it was okay. We could go," Alice informed the rest of them, in a very serious way for an eight-year-old. "Uncle Wayne looked kinda jumpy, like he *had* to go. And he was all red in the face." She nodded, as if she'd thought about her decision and agreed with it. "I wanted to help him."

"So we all got in my Toyota and drove up to the yellow gate, and wouldn't you know it, there's a truck parked there. And we both know it's Bob Doyle's truck, 'cause it has that blue tailgate. I get kinda angsty 'cause I don't want Bob seeing us drag out a dead deer. 'Where'd you put it?' I say to Wayne, meaning the deer. And he says it's down the logging road but it's okay 'cause Bob Doyle ain't around. He figures Bob's truck just broke down 'cause he hasn't seen him anyplace around. So I say, ‘Okay, let’s go get this deer,’ and he says, ‘No, no! You two wait in the truck.’ Something don’t feel right to me but Wayne’s gone before I can say nothing, and the next thing I know I see him dragging something out from behind some alders on the other side of this tree that’s fallen across the road.”

Lange looked across at Michelle; that must have been where the sheriff’s K9 marked the third place.

“Then we hear barking,” Alice chimed in. “Barking and barking and barking, and I say to my dad, ‘What’s that?’ And we see this little dog here”—she points to Max in her lap—“barking and jumping at Uncle Wayne. Jumping real high.” Alice put her right arm up above her shoulder to suggest how high the dog was jumping.

“‘Looks like Bob Doyle’s dog,’ I tell Alice,” Kyle continued. “Trying to get Wayne’s attention. Only he must’ve been making my brother mad, ’cause Wayne starts throwing rocks at him. But the dog keeps barking and leaping and making circles around him, and the next thing I see, Wayne pulls a pistol . . .”

“And shoots the dog!” finished Alice, her mouth wide with shock and indignation. “I hear a big yelp and then crying and then *I* start to cry . . .”

“So I get out of the truck and tell Alice to stay there, ’cause I can see her from where Wayne is, and I march up to him when he’s climbing over the tree and I yell, *‘What the . . .* ’” Kyle shot a quick look at Brandie and didn’t finish his sentence. “But that’s when I see that he don’t have no deer. And I say as much. ‘That don’t look like no deer,’ I say, pointing at this bag he’s got. Like a gym bag, only heavy. And he begs me, real panicked like, ‘Please, I’m already late with this delivery.’ And I say, ‘That’s drugs?!’ And now *I’m* real mad ’cause I don’t want no part of it if it’s drugs, and he *knows* that! And I’m getting ready to go back to the truck, but he grabs me and tells me he wouldn’t’a got me involved, only he had to talk Tosha into bringing him up to get the drop, ’cause his Jeep is broke down, and she wouldn't leave till she got herself ready for work, so they didn't even start up the hill till six and he was s'posed to have *been* here by then. And when they get up to the gate they see Bob Doyle's truck parked there, and Tosha gets real nervous and keeps driving up the road, Wayne telling her the whole time that it's stupid trying to hide from Bob Doyle. That if he's out there on the logging road, Wayne'll deal with him."

Now Michelle flicked a glance Lange's way; *sounds like our killer*, it seemed to say.

"Anyway, he finally convinces Tosha to drive him back to the gate, only she must've got nervous again after Wayne was outta sight, 'cause she took off. Just left him there. Wayne said he didn't even know she was gone until after he found the drugs and was on his way back to the rig. Then he didn't know what to do 'cept hide the drugs and walk down Sauk to my place to get my truck."

"Why didn't he walk the drugs out with him?" asked Suleka, confused by Wayne's logic. Or lack of logic.

"'Cause he was scared, that's what he told me. Scared someone would stop him and ask what's in the bag. 'But you're not scared they'll do the same to *me*!' I yell at him, and he tells me, 'If you'd'a just given me your truck like I wanted, you wouldn't *be* up here.'

"'Yeah, well, I'm not gonna be up here any longer,' I tell him, 'and you can go to *hell* with your drugs, 'cause I'm *not* driving you out with them.'" Kyle paused and his right hand found its way to his swollen lip. "So he punched me."

"I saw it," Alice confirmed. "And then Daddy fell down . . ."

"I musta hit my head against the tree and knocked myself out."

"He fell down and he didn't get up," said Alice, her eyes wide again. "I got real scared. Too scared even to cry. I wanted to go help Daddy but Uncle Wayne was at the truck and he threw that big bag in, and it thumped when it landed on the floor and made me jump. And then he started driving down the mountain real fast."

"The red Toyota that spun past you," Michelle said across to Lange.

He nodded. He wouldn't have seen Alice in the vehicle because she wasn't tall enough to have her head be above the back of the seat.

Alice continued. "I asked Uncle Wayne, 'But what about my dad?' and he said, 'Shut up! Just shut up!'" She said it forcefully, the way her uncle must have said it to her, and Kojak nudged her hand to be petted again. Alice stroked him, regaining her composure. "I didn't want Uncle Wayne mad at me. So I stayed quiet. And I stayed quiet the whole time, waiting for my dad to come get me."

"You did good, honey," said Kyle, pulling his daughter's head in close and kissing the top of it.

"Where did your uncle take you?" Michelle asked Alice.

"To his house."

"And when did *you* get there?" Lange asked Kyle.

"I don't know. I don't know how long she had to wait for me. I came to and they were gone. And all I could think of was I had to get Alice back. My head hurt and there was blood on my hand when I touched it, but I had to get to her. I *had* to." He looked like he might cry. He sucked in a big breath, filling his chest, and went on. "So I walked out to Bob Doyle's pickup, thinking maybe I could get it started even though it was broke down, and I found the keys, tried to start it—and it lit right up!" He said it like it was the biggest surprise of his day. "Finally a break, I thought. Except when I went to back it up, I saw you"—he pointed at Lange—"in the rearview mirror, coming up the road. You were looking, like, off to the side, so I didn't think you'd seen me but I couldn't risk it."

"Couldn't risk what?" asked Suleka.

"Him seeing me steal the truck! I woulda got caught and then Brandie woulda been mad at me . . ."

Brandie made a *pchuh!* of irritation and tossed her head up into the air. "You shoulda just told me," she muttered.

Kyle looked at her, then let it go. He continued with his narrative. "So I drove *up* the road instead of down, 'cause I didn't wanna go past him," he said, meaning Lange. "And I kept on driving to where I thought would be past where he walked. Then I waited."

"I never even saw the truck," Lange said, surprised at himself for not being situationally aware when he was usually so good about that. "You must not have been out for too long, because I'm guessing you saw me from the truck right after your brother blew me off the road."

"You must have been pretty mad," Suleka said to Lange. "Not to hear him start the truck."

"Well, he was a distance off," Kyle justified on Lange's behalf.

"But yes," Lange said in answer to Suleka. "I was pretty mad. I even thought about chucking a rock at the vehicle, that's how mad I was."

"I wish I'd got to him before he took off," said Kyle, stroking his daughter's hair.

Alice tapped his belly reassuringly and said, "It's okay, Daddy."

"How long did you wait up the mountain?" asked Lange.

"I don't know. It felt like forever. I didn't want you to see me but I had to get back to Alice, so I put myself in another place in my head, like Brandie taught me, to make myself wait."

"What other place?" asked Alice, curious. Lange was seeing the little girl in her reemerge, and he was glad that Clarkson had thought to make his confession this way.

"I went back to when you and your mom and me climbed Sauk when you was, like, three. And some lady who followed us up the trail told us the only reason she made it was 'cause she kept looking at you, thinking, 'If she can do it, I can do it.'"

"That's a lot of trail for a three-year-old," Suleka told Alice, impressed.

"I usually walk for about an hour, so you must have waited at least that long," Lange said, bringing them back to the subject.

Kyle shrugged. "Like I said, I don't know for sure. All I know is, my brother was pacing like a caged cougar when I pull into his place, saying as how he was tired of waiting with Alice and how he had to go deliver the drugs, like, right now."

"Did he say where?"

"No, 'cause I didn't ask! I didn't care. I just wanted my daughter and my truck, and when he figured out he wasn't gonna get to take my Toyota, he made a run for it in Bob's pickup."

Lange and Michelle made eye contact again. He left it in her hands to do the next part. "Well, Alice, you helped us a lot by telling us what happened, but now we need to talk to your dad alone. Could you maybe take the dogs outside, let them run around a bit?"

"Sure, we can do that," Brandie said, bouncing up and putting her hand out to encourage Alice to join her.

They left and Michelle gave the floor to Lange. "You've pretty much answered everything we wanted to know," he said to Kyle, "except one thing."

"What?"

"Was Kevin Doyle involved in picking up the drugs?"

"No. I don't think so." Kyle shrugged. "I mean, why would Wayne have needed Tosha if he was gonna go up with Kevin? Plus Kevin don't do those kind of drugs."

"What kind of drugs?" Michelle asked softly.

"Heroin." Kyle's eyes shifted from one to the other of them. "Isn't that what my brother was moving?"

Nobody answered.

"If Kevin wasn't there," said Lange, leaning forward slightly over the top of Suleka's head, "did your brother tell you why *Robert* Doyle was there?"

"He weren't there. Just his pickup was." He looked from one to the other of them again, his face cagey like he was sensing a trap. "Why?"

"Doyle's dog was there. You saw your brother shoot at him. Didn't you wonder why both the dog and the pickup were there but not Doyle himself?"

A look passed across Kyle's face, like this was the first time he'd thought about that. "No. But that is strange." His eyes narrowed, like his mind was catching up with Lange's questions.

"Did something happen to Bob?"

Suleka nodded. "Cal and Michelle found Doyle dead right next to where Kyle found the drugs."

"And you think . . . ? Nooooo. No, I don't think my brother would kill Bob Doyle. He does some bad stuff but killing . . . that don't sound like my brother."

"But what if he didn't mean to kill him?" asked Michelle. "He punched him the same way he punched you?"

"When would he have done that? When we was up there?"

"No, we're thinking earlier in the day, when he went up with Tosha."

"And that's why she took off? Is that what you're thinking?"

"It's a possibility."

"Yeah, but then why wouldn't he have just stole Bob Doyle's pickup to bring the drugs out? He knew Bob wouldn't need it and the keys were in it."

There was a pause as they all contemplated this. "You think he just didn't see the keys?" Michelle asked Lange.

"He punched me and when I went down, first thing he did was steal my truck. Didn't even bother him that Alice was in it. All he wanted was to get the hell outta there before I came to, so he could get the drugs someplace off the mountain."

"So if he'd knocked Bob down," Suleka posited, "and got back to the gate to see his ride had gone, he would have automatically looked to steal Bob's truck. That's what you're thinking?"

Kyle Clarkson nodded yes.

"Then why wouldn't he steal it if he just didn't know where Bob was?" she persisted.

"Maybe 'cause he was batshit mad at Tosha for leaving him there and didn't even think to look for the keys."

"Which were where?" asked Lange.

"Under the visor. That's where Bob always kept them."

"You knew that how?"

"From all the times me and Kevin took Bob's truck to go do

stuff in."

"Would Wayne have known that?" asked Michelle.

"I don't know. He wasn't as good a friend with Kevin as me."

"The thing is," said Lange, "Wayne could also have left the truck there deliberately, to put us off the track of him killing Bob Doyle."

Kyle rolled his eyes, and the look on his face suggested that this was way beyond anything his brother would think up. He added a headshake to his eye roll. "I just don't see it. If someone like Bob Doyle came at him, I'd see him cursing him out but hitting him? No way. He'd run, that's what he'd do. 'Cause he coulda run a lot faster than old Doyle." He sat forward on the couch and insisted on his point with Lange. "My brother's done a lot of bad stuff but he's not a killer. He's not. Look," he said, pointing out the door toward where Alice and Brandie had gone. "He coulda taken off with Alice and his drugs, down to make the delivery, but he didn't. He didn't even leave her at his place by herself. He waited till I got there and then he took off."

Brandie popped her head back in the door. "Detective Collins is out here for you," she said to Lange.

Lange broke eye contact with Clarkson. "Okay, we'll leave it there for now. But we'll be back," he said as Suleka and Michelle stood up to leave with him.

"Yeah, alright," moaned Kyle, lifting himself up off the couch.

Lange started to move the kitchen chair back to its rightful place.

"Here, I'll get that," Kyle offered.

"We found a check that belongs to you up on the road," Michelle put in before crossing to the door.

"You've got it?" asked Kyle, surprised. "I was looking for that so I could cash it." He stopped, his hands on the back of the chair, and Lange could see his mind turning over his movements up on the mountain to figure out how he dropped the check. It finally came to him. "Musta been when I pulled out my bandana to mop up the blood on my head." He put one hand out toward Michelle. "Can I have it?"

"It's with forensics," Michelle told him, shaking her head. "So not until they've finished with it, no."

Kyle gave them one more caustic eye roll before they all walked out.

Collins was waiting down on the street, and Lange could see he was feeling good. "You've got news," he said.

"I do," Collins replied. Michelle and Suleka came up to join them, and Collins glanced behind them all at Alice and Brandie, as if concerned about being overheard. "You want to do it here or . . ."

"Let's go back down to the park," suggested Lange.

"You ride with Collins," said Michelle, "and we'll gather up the dogs and follow you."

"Okay." Lange swung around and strode over to Alice. "Thank you," he said. "For all your help."

"Do the dogs have to go now?" she asked.

"They do," said Michelle. Lange gave Brandie a quick wave of thanks, too, and walked away, hearing Michelle say, "But maybe we can bring them back for another visit sometime."

Lange dropped in beside Collins in the Ford Interceptor.

"Did he tell you much?" asked the detective as he started them down the hill toward the park again.

"About the drugs, yes. And the fight he had with his brother because of them." Lange quickly recapped what Clarkson had told him. "But he said he didn't know anything about Robert Doyle except the fact that he wasn't up there."

Collins pulled into the same parking spot he'd taken earlier, in front of the cabin, and switched off the engine. "Well, I got some news from the pathologist on cause of death," he said, swinging away from Lange to get out of the car. Lange followed suit, stepping up onto the grass in front of the vehicle to walk around and join Collins.

Collins's cell phone rang and he reached into his jacket pocket, pulled it out, looked at the caller ID, and then held his index finger up to Lange—*just a sec.* He walked away as he answered the call.

Lange turned around to face the river. He took a deep breath, his chest expanding toward the fast-flowing current, his eyes closed as he tuned into the swirly lapping of the water against the bank. He thought back to Robert Doyle, his long, aging fingers stroking a piece of cedar that he'd just milled, proudly showing Lange the tight grain in the wood. The rich molasses-brown cedar had emitted a smell that put Lange in the woods even as he stood in the old fellow's yard. He tried to see Robert's face, to ask him what happened up there on Sauk, but his communing was interrupted by vehicles pulling in behind him.

He glanced back to see both Suleka and Michelle switching off their engines. They each climbed out, leaving the dogs in the vehicles, and walked over to join him on the grass. Collins finished his phone call and hurried over, his step buoyant, energized. "Wayne Clarkson's been picked up," he announced. "Burlington police saw Doyle's truck parked outside a bar down there and found Wayne Clarkson inside, drinking up his drug profits."

"Have they questioned him yet?" asked Michelle.

"No. They only just picked him up. That was the police chief letting me know they'd got him. He said Clarkson's pretty hammered. I'm going to head down now, be there ready for when he does sober up. There's just one thing," he said to them all as if he needed a favor so he could get going.

"Go ahead," said Lange.

"I heard from the pathologist. She said cause of death was the blow to the front of the head, which fractured Doyle's skull. Made by something heavy and flat, about six or eight inches wide, she guessed. So I wanted to go back up Sauk, look around and see if maybe there's a length of two-by-six, or a broken limb wide enough, close to where we found the body."

"We can do that," said Lange, gesturing to include Suleka. He looked at Michelle. "What are you going to do?"

"I want to be part of the interview with Clarkson but maybe I'll come with you first, and look for the murder weapon. If Clarkson did kill Doyle while he was executing a felony connected to the drug dealers, we might be able to use that as leverage to get him to give us their names." She looked at Collins. "But I'd rather not say that till we have proof Doyle was murdered."

"And that's my first interest," he told her. "The homicide. The drug bust I'll leave up to you."

CHAPTER 11

Ten minutes later, Lange was sitting in the Nissan again, his elbow propped on the open window, his mouth leaning on his knuckles as he stared out at the bank alongside Sauk Mountain Road. This time he wasn't looking through the trees, though; he was simply going over what Kyle Clarkson had told them as he let the warm wind blow through his mop of white hair.

Max sat tidily between Lange and Suleka, watching through the windshield as the truck labored up the road. "It's too bad you can't keep this little guy," said Suleka.

"Which little guy?" asked Lange out of one side of his mouth. He wasn't ready to pull away from his thoughts quite yet.

"Max."

"Oh." Lange dropped his hand and turned to look at the pup. "Yeah. But I do think René will want him." He ran his hand down the far side of the dog, feeling his bones and his belly through his soft, thin coat. "Maybe we'll go over there after we finish up here. That way we'll find out. Hopefully Kevin will still be there, too." He stared out the open window again. "I want to ask him some more questions."

"You do?"

"Uh-huh. I still can't make a case for Bob being up here without him having some prior knowledge of the drugs from Kevin. If you take Kevin out of the picture, I've got Wayne and Bob on an abandoned logging road with a gym bag." He turned toward Suleka, his thumb rubbing the top of Max's head. "What would make Bob think there were drugs in that gym bag? And if he didn't think that, why would he have confronted Wayne? And if he didn't confront Wayne, why did Wayne smack him with a two-by-six?"

"You're assuming that they both arrived at the gym bag at the same time. Wayne was late, that's what he told Kyle. So what if Bob

Doyle was up there, for whatever reason, got to the bag on the road ahead of Wayne, and opened it? Just serendipitously? Like you serendipitously noticing the brush was messed up when you went out there to look at the blackberries."

Lange's thumb stopped moving. He stared off in front of him, his mind racing, all the pieces of the puzzle suddenly making sense.

"And it's a good thing you did," said Suleka, pulling in beside Michelle's Range Rover at the yellow gate. "Otherwise Bob Doyle's body might never have been found."

But Lange wasn't hearing her. He was slipping the last piece of the puzzle into place as she switched off the engine. And in the sudden, peaceful quiet up on the side of the mountain, he saw Robert Doyle's gentle countenance smiling back at him.

"You've figured it out, haven't you?" said Suleka, recognizing the self-absorbed look on his face.

Lange didn't say a word. He rolled out of the Nissan, Max beside him, and drifted past Michelle toward the gate, almost trancelike.

Michelle jumped to fall in step beside him. "Are we going to organize how we hunt for this chunk of wood in this forest? Like each take a side?" she asked.

Lange strode ahead, oblivious to everything except finding the proof he now knew existed. Michelle glanced back at Suleka, who was moving down the road at a more sedate pace, and pulled both sides of her mouth down; *what's up?*

"Ignore him," said Lange's partner with a flap of her hand. "He'll tell us what he's figured out once he can show us."

"He's figured something out?"

Their conversation drifted into the background as Lange pushed on, picking Max up to carry him past the place where he'd been shot, then setting him back down. Both he and the dog threaded their way nimbly through the pearly everlastings and overgrown thistles, Lange's mind on Robert, in the distance, choosing places to put his feet so he could make it up the hillside. It would have been quiet, like now, abundantly peaceful, and undoubtedly cooler. And Bob would have been happy, tarrying with his dog, alone the woods.

The ex-detective raced to the spot where he'd stood sampling berries just yesterday morning: where Robert Doyle had lain at his feet without him even knowing it, where a bag of drugs weighing maybe sixty pounds or more had fallen from the sky, where this little cream-and-tan dog had watched his master come to an end. And Lange started his search. He looked past the smashed-down ferns and the wild cherry that had drawn his attention yesterday and scanned the hillside above. What would he be looking for? he asked himself. Something clear? Something white? Maybe something with writing on it. Maybe something that he couldn't see from down here.

He stepped his right foot across the ditch, wedged it behind the base of a small alder, and hopped across, placing his left foot on a rock jutting out of the bank. He leaned his weight on the rock and leveraged himself uphill a few steps in the soft, dry duff. Now that he was this close, he could just make out the tracks in the dirt. There was a swath of vines, thick with berries, a few feet above his head, and two obvious toeholds that someone had used to stand there and pick, but Lange didn't think he needed to climb that high to find what he was looking for.

His eyes traveled slowly, exhaustively over and around the ferns, grasses, and brambles, waiting for it to pop out at him. Behind him, he could hear Michelle and Suleka getting closer, and beside him, he heard a scuffling sound in the brush. He looked around and saw Max scrabbling his way up the hillside. Lange explored the dirt where Max was climbing, wondering if what he was looking for had been dropped in the incident, but no luck.

He turned his head to look uphill again; start at the top and work your way down, he told himself. He searched for a flat spot close to the toeholds but didn't find it. Maybe he should go higher, he thought. He stepped up, digging his feet into the soil, hearing grains of it tumble down through the brush below him. He got to eye level with the toeholds, stroking Max, who was already there, ahead of him, sniffing the ground with alacrity. Lange looked left and right, then wrapped his fingers around a length of mossy vine maple and hoisted himself up to straddle Max. Wild blackberries hung in front of his face like jewels on a braided vine, and to their right, nestled in the crook of some spraying sword ferns, was a dark-gray thirty-two-ounce water bottle. The lid was open, and Lange could see the bottle was two-thirds full of blackberries.

"What are you doing?" came Suleka's voice from behind him. "I thought we were looking for a murder weapon, not picking blackberries."

Lange found a narrow, cigar-length stick of vine maple with a fork at the end of it, reached across, and hooked the plastic fingerhold on the lid of the water bottle. He lifted it up into the air and said, "This is what Bob Doyle was doing up here."

CHAPTER 12

They stood on the road together, Kojak chasing Max in and out of the ditch as Lange described what must have happened. "You were right," he told Suleka at the beginning. "Bob Doyle got here ahead of Wayne Clarkson. He might even have been here as early as five a.m., who knows, so he'd beat the heat in the slow, methodical process of picking these tiny blackberries. And while he was up there"—he nodded his chin up toward the blackberry patch—"perched on the hillside, a small plane flew overhead. He must have looked up, wondering what it was doing flying so low, and the bag of drugs dropped smack on his forehead, knocking him backward down into the ditch, where he landed on the rock. It was his body that disturbed the brush, not the drugs, which must have bounced off him and down onto the road. Wayne Clarkson had no idea that Bob Doyle was lying dead just a few feet away when he came to retrieve the bag. No more than I did when I came to investigate the ripeness of the berries." He turned and looked into the eyes of his friend and partner; they were full of sadness. "I'm glad, like you said, that I had a hankering for berries yesterday."

"Yeah," Suleka agreed. She let her gaze drift back up the hillside, to where Bob Doyle had been picking. "At least he was doing something he loved."

They stood in silence for a moment, then Lange looked at Michelle. "So what's next?" he asked.

"I want to get the dealers," she commented, her mouth tight with anger. "And prosecute them for a felony homicide."

Lange nodded, feeling the same anger. He swung around and started leading them all back toward the yellow gate. "Are you going to offer Clarkson a deal on the drug charge if he gives up the suppliers?"

"That's my plan."

"Maybe do it without telling him about Doyle's death. Then Collins might be able to tie him into the homicide, too."

The idea obviously appealed to Michelle, because Lange saw the anger clear from her jaw. "Good thinking," she said, stretching out ahead of him. "I'm going to go call Collins right now and tell him. Hopefully I'm not too late."

Lange watched her jog down the road and smiled when the dogs ran to catch up with her, then glanced right, thinking Suleka might have seen him. But her eyes were firmly fixed on the road ahead of them.

"I remember Bob used to sell some of the berries he picked to local bakeries," said his friend and partner. They stopped in front of the fir, and Lange put his hand out for her to hold as she climbed over it. "I wonder if that's where 5b's got the berries for their bumbleberry pies?"

"Did you eat those?" asked Lange. He followed her across the fir.

"No, they're still in the car."

"Good. I was hoping I might get one of those."

"Let's take them back to your yurt," suggested Suleka. "Have a little coffee and bumbleberry pie as a tribute to Bob."

"I like that idea," agreed Lange. "I wonder if Michelle has time to join us before she goes down to interview Clarkson?"

"I don't know," said Suleka. "Maybe you should ask."

And Lange thought he caught a twinkle of mischief in her eye before she turned away from him to go around the yellow gate.

CHAPTER 13

Clarkson was still sleeping off his drunk, according to Detective Collins, so Michelle followed them to Lange's property. Suleka watched them from the Nissan, standing side by side in the afternoon sunlight, pointing at the snow-topped mountain ridges opposite and the sinewy curl of the Skagit River below. She'd never seen Cal so comfortable in the company of a woman—in the company of anyone, if she were to be honest—and now here he was, showing off the view from his place to someone who got the magic of it.

She climbed out of the Nissan slowly, deliberately, and walked around to the back. She unlatched the canopy window and lifted it to get out the small cooler.

"Are you coming?" she heard Lange say as she was leaning into the bed.

She pulled her head out, cooler in hand, latched the window closed again, and walked around to join him alongside the Nissan. Michelle was still over by his log pile, facing toward them now, shading her eyes with her hands as she looked at the craggy top of Sauk above them.

Suleka put on her best regretful face. "I just got a call from one of the women in my spinning group, and she needs me to go check on her goats."

"Uh-huh," said Lange, like he didn't believe a word of it. "I thought your cell phone didn't get service up here?"

"Er, well, you know," sputtered Suleka, "sometimes it does."

"Is that right?" He leaned in closer and whispered, "You forget I used to be a detective."

Suleka laughed. She thrust the cooler into his hands. "Go enjoy the pies with your guest."

"If you say so," he acquiesced, grateful for her kindness. "And what will you do? Really?"

Suleka slipped her hands in the pockets of her overalls, thinking about his question. She could see the amber in Kojak's coat catching the sunlight as he chased Max around the log pile. "I think I may go sit with René Doyle awhile," she said. "See if she wants Max to go back to her or stay up here on the mountain, close to Bob."

He was watching the dogs, too, feeling an unexpected fondness for the quick-moving terrier eluding the German shepherd. "Maybe we can arrange it for him to do both," he said.

"Mmmmm," reflected Suleka. "Maybe." She pulled the keys to the Nissan out of one pocket and jiggled them. "Well, you go have fun," she said, walking away from Lange. "And don't spend your whole time trying to find another lame word to beat me with in Scrabble."

"I thought that was a great word!" he exclaimed, tossing his arm in the air.

"Is that right?" she said. She leaned back toward him and whispered, "You forget I'm better than you at games."

Then she headed around the Nissan, chuckling.